- I, ...ADOW BOOK ONE -

# THE
# STARS
## BEYOND THE
# MESA

## PETE A O'DONNELL

First Printing, 2020

ISBN: 978-1-7349090-0-5

Ill-Advised Stories **PO** Box 6072   Warwick, RI 02887 www.illadvisedstories.com

## Dedication

To my dad, my first reader.

Thank you for watching X-files, Star Trek, Dr. Who, Star Wars and Battlestar with me, and for pushing me to visit the vast universes that can only be found in books.

## Also by
Pete A O'Donnell

In the Giant's Shadow Book two: The Ocean Beyond

The Adventures of Sparkie and Sapzoid: Portal's World

The Curse of Purgatory Cove

# Chapter One

The sky was bright with stars shinning down on an empty desert. Katy thought about the art supplies in her bag, wondering if she'd ever be able to capture a night like this, the way the Milky Way formed a river of light. She wasn't much of a painter. She tried but she was better with pencils. 'I'll have to use shades of grey and white,' she thought as she composed in her head even though there wasn't time.

She took another careful step down the hillside. Something moved, leaving a trail of dust across the rocky soil. A rabbit darting away. It reminded her that this place wasn't empty and that she didn't trust it. The stars may be pretty, but they made shadows on the barbed bushes and sand-blasted stones, dark places where venomous things hid, rattlesnakes, scorpions and other terrible creatures waiting in ambush.

Behind her, a pale dome stuck out from the side of a high bluff like a swollen sore on the top of the mesa. It didn't seem all that different from the observatory at Kitt's Peak six hours to the south, but it was.

A dark scar marked its white surface where there'd been an explosion a few nights before. Katy didn't know much about telescopes, but she was certain they didn't explode or shake the ground the way this one did. Occasionally they were supposed to open and look at the stars. This one never had.

Katy was too far down the hill to see the fences, buildings, and trailers that'd been her home for the last few weeks. She wasn't going to miss any of it.

Watching her footing, she thought, 'it'd be a shame to turn back because of a twisted ankle.' Not far away, a dirt road cut up the side of the mesa, bending and turning like a snake, as it followed the slope. That's where she was heading to meet Troy, her sort-of boyfriend.

Troy tried hard enough, but she refused to formally call them a couple. Tonight was a prime example. He'd driven hours from San Diego to help her escape. He'd been two years ahead of her in high school, graduating this June, but that didn't matter, because according to her dad, Katy was too young to date anyone. Good thing the professor was never around.

For two years her father had been out here in the desert, building this place while she and her brother Ben stayed with family. Ben had proven to be too much to handle for their aunt. He'd probably be too much for an entire marine detachment. Her little brother had issues, but he had his uses too. He was the one who found the hole in the fence making tonight's escape possible.

She looked down, seeing the headlights of Troy's truck parked off to the side of the road. 'What am I doing' played in her head like a broken record. 'True, she no longer wanted to be marooned in the desert, and true, she liked Troy, but was she really running off with him?' She shook her head, 'no. That's not what this was.' She thought of her aunt, wondering if she could convince her to let her stay with her again. Honestly, the only reason her dad wanted Katy out here was to take care of Ben.

She was a babysitter for a fifteen-year-old that her dad had no idea how to deal with him.

Katy got low, sitting on her backside as gravel tumbled under her while she scooted down the last stretch of hill. She got to her feet on the dirt road that was better suited for horses, dusting herself off as she walked towards the truck.

It was such a quiet night that all she could hear was the gravel still slipping behind her. She approached the truck, wondering why Troy hadn't gotten out yet. Maybe he was asleep. His pick-up was small and old with 4X4 blazoned across the tailgate.

Katy squeezed between the hill and the truck's side. When she got to the cab, she looked inside and found it empty. The window was down and the faint scent of an air freshener came out, along with a whiff of body spray. Honestly, she didn't understand why guys wore that stuff.

She looked around, wondering if Troy had gone to take a leak or something. Then she touched the hood, feeling the heat from the still warm engine. "Troy are you out here?" she called.

There was no place for him to hide if this was some sort of joke. Katy reached in, shutting off the lights, not wanting the battery to die. She noticed the keys weren't in the ignition.

It was easier to see without the headlights on, though she had to wait, getting used to the dark and starlight again. She noticed another light in the distance. A faint, shimmering glow hovering low over the ground further around and up the hill from her.

The glowing object never held still, diving and ducking around the boulders and gullies on the rockier

3

side of the slope. For a moment she thought it might be a drone, but who'd be dumb enough to fly one of those in the dark so close to the ground. The light didn't travel far, but it was intense, a small point like the afterglow of a torch, like a fading spark in her eye.

Mesmerized by the way it seemed to dance over the sandy soil, she watched it for a moment, then she noticed someone going towards it. 'Could that be Troy?' She wondered. He struggled up the hill, tripping and falling on the rougher terrain.

She called again, more forcefully this time, "Troy!"

He didn't turn his head, didn't make any motion to show that he'd heard her. He kept moving towards the light as it traveled up the slope, back toward the facility.

Katy was going to yell again, even louder but something told her not to. She wasn't sure why she didn't want her voice to carry. Maybe it was the glowing object that was so beautiful, bizarre and strange. The hairs on the back of her neck stood up as she felt watched.

Katy thought of her father and of the observatory dome, the way it hummed, the way it never opened. The way he didn't talk about his work and how he'd made excuses the night of the explosion.

After a deep breath, she started back up the hill, bending over and using her hands to guide her over the steep spots. Taking her time, she climbed across the slope, carefully crossing into the rockier area, moving faster than Troy. He didn't seem to be paying any attention to his footing, lumbering ahead, stumbling and getting up again.

Before long, Katy was close behind him. She noticed he was wearing his hoodie from their high school track team, but he wasn't moving like any sort of athlete. His steps were slow and deliberate, as if he were walking for the first time.

Up ahead, the ground glowed with shades of pink, blue and green, sometimes turning bright white. There was a sound too, a low fluttering as the glowing thing darted about quickly, staying too low to the ground for her to see what it was.

"Troy," she called almost in a whisper, coming up behind him.

There was still no reaction, so she tried again,

"Troy. Troy, I'm right here."

Katy put her hand on his shoulder as he kept walking, grabbing his sweatshirt. He jerked his arm forward, pulling it away.

"Hey," she said, grabbing again, this time pulling, trying to twist him towards her. He finally looked back and Katy gasped. There was something wrong with him. Something so incredibly strange. Frozen with shock, unable to understand what she was seeing, she stared at her friend.

Where she expected to see his deep brown eyes, there was a faint glow, a white light seeping out from under half-closed eyelids. His face was slack. It showed no emotion. Those glowing eyes opened wider and looked at her hand still on his shoulder. He took it harshly and flung it away, then shoved her.

Katy fell back, grabbing a handful of thorny weeds to keep from sliding down the hill. She was stunned by what she'd seen, but the rough landing and the stabbing thorns helped clear her thoughts.

She looked up at Troy and saw him start to climb again, moving a little quicker, as if trying to make up for lost time. He stumbled and floundered as he reached a steeper part of the slope. Staying on his hands and knees he climbed on.

The glow was just over the rise, coming close to the facilities security fence. Katy watched Troy get further away, not sure what to do, certain that she was in some sort of dream. The buzzing faded into the distance. All she could hear was the sound of Troy's struggling steps.

There was another noise. A thump followed by footsteps moving quickly, crunching in the soil. Something else was hurrying through the dark, something large and frightening. Katy's eyes searched, trying to find it. Then her attention fell on a dark spot, blacker than the night, on the rise just before the fence, moving quickly towards Troy. It was like a shadow come to life. She felt trapped watching it, hearing its feet sweeping through the sand.

The dark thing stalked her friend. It took the last few yards with a speed that seemed impossible for its size, then it sprang off the ledge, and fell on him.

Katy held her breath watching him go down. 'I should do something,' she thought. She started to her feet, trying to control her panic, still not understanding what was happening. As she took a single step forward, the shadow raised a long appendage, a curved claw at the end of a sinuous arm. It was a dark silhouette against the stars. The attacker brought the arm down on Troy, pinning him to the ground.

The young man struggled, kicking his legs and fighting helplessly. Katy saw the creature's head rear up. It was wide and as black as the rest of the thing. Like the arm, she could only see its edges against the stars. The head came down again and something shot from its mouth. Troy's scream was brief, filled with terror then the night went silent again.

Katy started backing away. The hill was a terrible place to run, but she tried. Falling, rolling and crawling down the hill, she managed to stop herself just before Troy's truck.

Getting to her feet, she looked back, trying to find the shadow thing, hoping it wasn't following her. Her eyes found the glowing object, up in the sky, flying away, dancing in front of the stars. There was a black spot below it, moving along the ground, that kept pace with the thing in sky, leaving Troy's body behind.

Katy took a deep breath, attempting to control her shaking. She wanted to call for help but she was still worried about raising her voice, wondering what could be out here listening. It took every bit of nerve she had to start back up the slope towards Troy. 'Please don't let those things come back,' she thought.

When she found him, he was face down. Katy couldn't tell if he was breathing. His skin was icy cold.

## Chapter Two

Alex was looking at his cell phone. "Well, I guess it was pointless bringing this," he said from the back seat. Outside, the broad expanse of the four corners region moved past the windows of the SUV. They were in the only vehicle on the road, and it had been that way for over an hour.

"We've got landlines at the facility and a secure Wi-Fi network," the driver said.

"Awesome," Alex answered with little enthusiasm, staring at the back of the man's head.

"We're only going to be here for a few weeks, a couple of months at the outside. Are you going to have a chip on your shoulder the whole time?" His mom looked back. Her blond hair was tied back, and her sunglasses hid her blue eyes. She was over forty but appeared younger, too young to have two teenage boys.

Staring out the window, Alex didn't answer. With his father's dark skin, he couldn't look more different from his mother.

"Your brother doesn't seem to mind. Right, Chris?" she said.

Chris looked up from his book, the second novel he'd read since flying out of Virginia. "What?"

"I said you don't seem to mind being out here."

Chris looked out the window at the sandstone rocks and blue skies going on forever. They were steadily climbing, making his ears pop. "Actually, I think it's kind of pretty."

"Well, you can have it," Alex said.

Chris closed his book and looked at the craggy stone face of a cliff that dwarfed everything around it.

At the top was the white dome of an observatory. "Since when did you start consulting on astronomy?" he asked his mom.

"I don't usually. I'm just doing a favor for an old friend."

As they got closer, the dome grew to the height of a six-story building and was nearly as wide, glistening in the sunlight, sitting on a broad pedestal surrounded by trailers, a few buildings, and a tall fence. "Wow, huh?" their mom said. "I can't believe he got all this together."

"Who do you mean?" Chris asked, noticing something wrong with the dome. There was an opening in it, a crack that ran down the side nearly splitting it apart like an eggshell. Men, working on a platform hung down from the top, lowered and placed massive steel plates over the opening like giant metal bandages. 'What could've done that,' Chris wondered. The edges of the crack looked ragged, blasted out from the inside.

"My friend Dr. Virtanen. We studied together years ago," his mom answered.

"He's an astronomer?"

"No, he's a theoretical physicist, like me."

Chris pointed to the dome. "I don't get it then."

"Astronomers and physicist work together all the time," she said.

"Some maybe, but not ones like you. You know the ones who work for the—" Chris was cut off by Alex punching him in the arm.

"Shut it, dude," Chris's older brother said, pointing with his eyes towards the driver.

"Alex don't hit your brother and Chris, you'll need a degree and clearance before I could explain it to you," his mom said, giving him a familiar face. The one she used every other time he'd asked about her work.

They pulled up to a large gate and a squat little building. The driver parked the SUV and said, "You're going to have to go in and get badges and what not. I'll be waiting out here."

The two boys and their mom entered the security office through a glass door, feeling a blast of air conditioning. There was a desk inside with a man in uniform sitting in front of a bank of monitors. Behind the desk were small offices. While his mom spoke to the guard, Chris wandered back a little, looking for the bathroom.

A harsh, threatening voice echoed down the hall. He glanced around the corner, looking through an open door to see a girl sitting in a small room. The lights above her were obnoxiously bright, shining down into her eyes. She was dirty, and there were tears on her face, but she glared defiantly across the room. Her skin was red and flushed with rage and she was in the middle of yelling. "I've already told you—" She stopped, caught sight of Chris, and stared in surprise.

Someone in the room stepped in front of the door blocking her from view. "We're not finished with this yet." The man stepped out into the hall, closing the door behind him, moving towards Chris. Tan with a thick mustache, he wore the gray shirt and black slacks of one of the security men. His wiry, thick muscles popped out under his polo. Even his face seemed to be well conditioned as it twisted into something that wasn't quite a smile.

He eyed Chris, stepping past and turning to Chris's mom. "You must be Dr. Johnson? We've been expecting you."

"What's going on back there?" Chris's mom asked, pointing to the door where the girl was. She'd heard the voices as well. "Is that Dr. Virtanen's daughter?"

"We had an incident last night. Nothing for you to worry about. I'm Mr. Pacheco, head of security." He put his hand out with that same twisted, almost painful smile.

Dr. Johnson was reaching out to take the hand when Alex called, "Hey, what are they doing out there?" He pointed towards the SUV. Two more security men were outside. They'd taken the family's luggage out of the trunk and were going through it. They were pulling Alex's baseball bag apart, laying the contents on the ground.

"What are they doing with our stuff?" Alex asked.

Pacheco looked out the window, then back at Dr. Johnson. "I'm sorry, but it's standard protocol for all new arrivals. X-ray machines are unreliable here."

They could hear the sound of Alex's aluminum bats bouncing off the ground. "Mom!" he demanded.

Dr. Johnson saw her clothes removed from her bag. "I'm sorry, but this is unacceptable. Stop them now."

"Dr. Johnson, it's protocol," Pacheco repeated.

"And who wrote those protocols?" A man with a thick red beard, ruddy skin, and the slight hint of an accent asked as he stepped into the office.

"Jonas, it's good to see you," the boy's mom said, going over and giving this new arrival a hug.

"It is good to see you too, Ellen." He hugged her back. Chris was still trying to place where the man was from, but it was hard to tell. His English was spoken in a precise manner. Chris guessed he was from somewhere in Northern Europe, Swedish maybe.

She turned to her sons saying, "Boys, this is Dr. Virtanen, the friend I was telling you about. He's in charge here."

Virtanen nodded to the boys, then turned to Pacheco. "There is no need to search the Johnson's things. I vouch for them. Please put their belongings back in the car and have them escorted to their quarters."

Pacheco starred at Virtanen coldly. "Doctor, that's not your decision." He looked out the window where his men were shoving things back into the bags.

"They're almost done anyway."

"Mr. Pacheco—" Virtanen started to say.

Pacheco ignored him, turning to the boys and their mom. "I'm going to need each of you to step in front of the camera." He indicated a digital camera set up, pointing at a clear piece of wall.

Dr. Johnson glanced out the window again. She turned to Virtanen, who shrugged apologetically. She nodded, stepping in front of the camera.

They were photographed and fingerprinted, then issued badges. Pacheco looked on silently while they finished the processing. Then Dr. Virtanen escorted them out to the car where the driver waited. He'd been one of the men going through the bags. Alex took a moment to glare at him while Chris climbed back in, rolling his window down.

Virtanen opened the door for their mother. She climbed in and looked back as he said, "I am sorry about this, Ellen. Pacheco is new and a bit enthusiastic. Given what we are dealing with, I do hope you can understand."

"I'm used to it. It's just strange for the boys," she answered.

"I have a few more things to deal with here, but I will meet you later," Virtanen said, giving her arm an affectionate squeeze. "I am really so happy you came."

Chris noticed the touch on his mother's arm, then looked back at the security office. He glanced at Pacheco, who stood out in front scowling.

He watched Virtanen's smile disappear as he approached the security head. Chris heard the scientist ask, "Where is she?" as he went back to the security office.

# Chapter Three

The Four Corners astronomical research facility sat on thirty acres of land on a wind-whipped mesa above the Painted Desert. It could only be seen from one side with tall rocks covering it in shadow during the hottest part of the day.

The observatory sat in the far northern corner of the facility, on a small rise, dwarfing the trailers and prefabricated buildings set up as housing around it. There were only a couple of permanent buildings, the large generator complex with its maintenance garages and oversized diesel tanks, and the community center with a cafeteria that also housed a medical facility. The buildings were made from corrugated steel and cinderblock, having been constructed for efficiency rather than aesthetics.

"It looks like a trailer park," Alex said as they drove down a lane of hard packed dirt and gravel.

"A lot of these are vacant. Left over from construction," the driver said. "We've tried to move as many people as we could towards the community center." He pointed to the long, low, metal building. "There's a computer room in there and a few ping pong tables."

He pulled up in front of a trailer that looked exactly like every other one. "This'll be yours. It's a two bedroom. There's some bigger housing on the other side, but Dr. Virtanen keeps those for the permanent staff. Like the Patels. You'll meet their daughter tomorrow in school," he said, looking back over the seat at the boys.

"Wait, what do you mean school?" Chris asked.

"Well, between you two, his kids and the Patel's daughter, Dr. Virtanen thought it'd be smart to get a tutor out here for you all. He set up one of the empty trailers as a classroom," the driver explained.

Alex and Chris both looked at their mom, who could only shrug. "You've got to have something to do with your time?" she said.

"I can think of plenty else," Alex shot back.

Chris was busy looking up at the observatory. They were close enough to where he could see the arc from welding torches on the metal plates covering the rip in the dome's surface, but the blue light was only a distraction from something else. He stared at the rocky peaks behind the dome and wondered why they would build the observatory in front of them. The whole point of one of these telescopes was to turn 360 degrees and see the whole night sky. By building this instrument where it was, they had lost almost half of their range. It didn't make sense. Chris looked at his mom ready to ask more questions, but then he thought better of it, knowing what her answer would be.

He could tell she was excited. Something here had piqued her interest. Given what she usually worked on, he had to wonder what it could be.

∞

Dr. Virtanen followed Pacheco back into the security office after the Johnsons left. "I saw the body at the medical office."

"I know, I've already been there. He's just like the other one," Pacheco said, standing behind his desk.

"Did you recognize the kid?"

Dr. Virtanen shook his head.

15

"He's a friend of your daughter. He was wearing a shirt from her high school." Pacheco looked down at some papers on his desk, going quiet, waiting for Virtanen to volunteer information. Finally, he looked up. "Do you have any idea how she managed to direct him here? How she managed to get him to a supposedly secret facility?"

"We are not all that secret," Dr. Virtanen said.

"Our purpose is supposed to be. Yet your daughter is inviting high school kids here. I said when I became head of security that our computer networks needed to be protected, no more casual use, business only. Now you've got this new family and more kids running around. What are you thinking?"

"I need Ellen. Everything we've created all the theories that our work is based on are hers. She wasn't coming out here without her family, now was she?"

"Does she know the danger they might be in?"

"I will tell her, but only after I show her. She needs to see what we have created. Then she will understand." Virtanen shook his head and looked at the door where his daughter was. "I'm more concerned with how Katy made it outside the fence. You're supposed to have this place secure. Explain to me how a teenage girl got out."

"I have men going over the fence now," Pacheco said.

Virtanen walked towards the closed door. "You should've called me as soon as you found her. How long has she been here?" He tried to turn the knob and found it locked.

"Just long enough to ask a few questions," Pacheco answered.

"That is unacceptable," Virtanen snarled at the man. "Now get over here and open this door. Let her out now."

Silently Pacheco took his keys, pushing past Virtanen. As the door opened, Katy's eyes met her dad's.

"Come on. We are going home." Virtanen waved her over and took her by the arm as they went back to the exit.

Pacheco called behind them, "I'm going to be setting new passwords for the network. I don't want them passed out to these kids."

"Very well," Virtanen said and followed his daughter outside.

Katy muttered, "Yeah, cause that'll keep us safe."

Virtanen ignored her comment, letting the door close behind them. When they were halfway across the parking lot, he grabbed her shoulder, pulling her back. "Staying inside the fence would have kept you safe."

Katy jerked her arm away, storming off, but then she turned back to him and asked, "Who were those kids? Who else did you bring out here?"

"They're a colleague's children. Don't worry about them," he said as he caught up.

"Don't worry about them? There's a monster out there attacking people. It attacked Troy. I don't know if he's alive or dead."

Virtanen looked at her for a moment as if he wanted to say something, but he shook his head with a sigh.

"What is it? Is he alive? Dad, you have to tell me. He's my friend!" she pleaded.

Virtanen shook his head. "It is complicated. I will not say any more than that, not before we do some testing."

Katy stared at her father for a moment, waiting for him to continue, but he stayed silent, not meeting her gaze.

"Yeah, everything's just fine," she said, storming off.

Virtanen didn't bother trying to catch up as he called behind her, "Stay inside the fence!" Then he whispered to himself, "You should be safe there."

# Chapter Four

Only a few miles from the facility, down a rutted dirt trail, was a crack in the face of a canyon wall, a narrow slit that was hard to see unless someone knew to look for it.

Millennia of flash floods made this opening. Heavy rains from the monsoon season sheared the sandstone away, making a slot canyon. Its walls climbed nearly a hundred feet high and were as narrow as a man's shoulders in places, while in other spots the walls spread to twenty feet or more. They were rubbed by wind and water as they twisted and turned, rising high over the soft, sand-covered floor. The smoothed-out ridges of earth glowed with a golden light as the blazing sun streamed down to touch them. There was a ledge forty feet above the ground, and on that ledge, someone was working.

His name was Tearmai, and he wasn't from this world. He was examining an octahedron, a massive piece of crystal, the size of a small car that had formed like a diamond. His long arm, thickly armored with dark scales, stretched out, touching the crystal's side with a clawed hand. Tiny tufts of black fur lined each of those scales. The exhaustion he felt after dragging the diamond vessel here nearly overtook him.

The crystal was damaged after crashing a few miles away. It'd been guided before, held by hands of living energy and flame. The creature was more concerned with the seals. If he couldn't get the crystal hatches to close tight, then there wouldn't be another passage, and he'd be stuck here.

He took tools from a small pouch and smashed his hand into the wall, splintering off pieces of the rock. 'The rocky soil wasn't the best material, but it'd have to' do, he thought as he lit a torch that was almost too small for him to hold. Bending over, he went to work while his mind tried to hold onto what he knew. Processing things this quickly was uncomfortable for him. It was all slipping away. He'd touched the void, seen how it was all laid out, how it would happen, and he knew it had to be stopped. There was something awful coming.

∞

Siting on her bed with her sketchpad in her lap, Katy was mad at herself. She couldn't believe she cried in front of that Pacheco guy. Given the night she had, it was understandable, but she hated being that girl. The one that got all emotional when something bad happened. Of course, calling what happened to her, or more specifically what happened to Troy, bad was a bit of an understatement. She tried getting some sleep, but it was tough. Her head wouldn't stop going over it all.

She'd only met Pacheco once before all this. He was new here. She thought about how he'd locked her in that office while she was blubbering, confessing what she'd seen. He was supposed to help, but all he did was stare at her like she was a bug, something to be squashed.

Again and again, he asked his questions, it was the same things; 'What did they look like? What did you see?' Her answers never changed. She couldn't tell him what the creatures looked like, because one was too dark and the other, it sounded silly, but it was too bright.

Of course, she could easily describe Troy. She'd never forget the blank stare on his face with his eyes glowing, or how he looked after the thing was done with him. There had been no choice but to leave him in the desert to go get help. He was too heavy to carry. She'd ran to the security office and pounded on the door. The men there followed her back to Troy's body.

"Is he dead?" she'd asked.

The man leaning over him looked up at her and said, "I think I found a pulse but it's faint." Then he used his radio to call in a medical team.

Dr. Wallace, the facility's medical director, came out with the team for Troy. Katy didn't like the skinny, young doctor any more than Pacheco. In a lot of ways, he was a bigger creep. He climbed the hill to look at her friend's body, then he questioned Katy, quick and pointedly while continuing his examination.

He collected samples from Troy's clothing and took pictures. "Aren't you going to help him?" Katy asked.

"We are, we are," the doctor assured her, but she didn't believe him. He was more interested in satisfying his curiosity, not trying to save anyone.

After the explosion, Dr Wallace and Pacheco had arrived at the facility within a day of each other. Katy couldn't decide which one was worse. The pencil nearly snapped on her sketchpad as she imagined Wallace examining Troy. She could picture her friend laid out on a cold table, that doctor more interested in studying him than in helping.

"What'cha you doing?" Ben asked from the door.

"Leave me alone," Katy said, looking up at her little brother. His hair was a fiery red bush of un-kept curls, sticking up everywhere.

He was already in the door and glancing over her hand at the pad. "What's that?" he asked, staring at what

21

she'd drawn. Katy had killed almost an entire pencil spreading black graphite over the page, shading the rocks, giving them texture. She'd created the stars just as she planned, but there was something in front of them.

It was the creature. Its form was vague. Katy hadn't seen enough to draw details.

She covered the pad and stared with venom at her brother. Ready to yell at him, she suddenly stopped. "Ben, what the hell did you do to your eyes?"

He reached up and touched where his eyebrows used to be. "Oh, yeah. I was playing with Dad's razor, the electric one. I think I went too far." The ridge above each of his eyes was completely bare.

Ben saw the look on his sister's face. "Does it look weird?" he asked.

Despite everything, all the horrible stuff she'd seen last night, Katy couldn't help laughing. She shook her head, then nodded. "It's not the weirdest thing I've seen. Close though."

# Chapter Five

'Hazel Hadley, the tutor, could've been from another planet,' Chris thought, listening to the man explain the differences between chunks of rock. He was overly narrow for someone so tall, and his movements were strangely fluid like he was doing a dance routine to music that only he could hear.

Chris, Alex, Ben and a girl were in a trailer with the teacher. The empty box was left over from the facility's construction. It was an open space, without walls to divide it into rooms. As the tutor stood in front of a white board, explaining the processes that created a piece of petrified wood, Chris felt a tap on his shoulder.

"Hey," Ben whispered. The pale, freckled kid was close to Chris's age. Alex and Chris had both done a double take when he wandered into the classroom late. They were unable to ignore Ben's drawn on eyebrows. It was even harder to ignore him because he kept tapping on Chris's shoulder.

"Hey," Ben said.

Chris shook his head.

Tap, tap, "Hey."

"What?" Chris demanded, turning around. Hadley crossed his arms, looking like he wanted to throw his fancy rock at his student.

Alex had been sitting silently through the entire lecture, looking angry, but still attentive. Chris thought his brother's intense gaze was bothering Hadley, who avoided Alex's side of the room. "What's your problem, Chris?" Alex growled.

Chris threw up his arms, motioning to Ben.

"Mr. Johnson, I am not fond of having my lectures interrupted. If you won't give me some modicum of respect, then at least show some concern for your classmates. Take poor Miss Patel here." The tutor pointed to the girl, Amita. She looked younger than Chris by a few years. Her black hair was tied up above her soft brown skin in a silk scarf. She sat up looking quizzical, with bright, green eyes.

Hadley continued, "She is far more intelligent than the rest of you, but yet she puts up with me dumbing down my lectures so you and your fellows can follow along. If she can pay attention, then I'm certain you should be able to muster enough focus to last until lunch."

Chris's face turned bright red. He looked around the room, trying to find an ally. Alex still looked mad. Ben, he wanted to punch, and Amita, she was smiling. Maybe it was because the teacher had said she was the one person with a brain in a room full of morons, but it didn't seem that way. It was more like she was amused by Chris's predicament. She cocked her head and held her hands up.

At lunch, Professor Hadley released the children on their 'own recognizance' with the attitude of a jailer who'd given criminals a brief parole.

As soon as Hadley left the room, Alex was up and moving, looking back at the others, muttering, "This is ridiculous," as he went to the door.

"Wow, dude, your brother seems angry," Ben said.

"Yeah, that's kind of his thing," Chris agreed as he turned in his seat. "He can be sort of intense." With his chair pushed back he looked around at the trailer. It might've been more barren than the one they were staying in, but not by much. He pictured going back there with his brother in a cranky mood. He shrugged turning to Ben, an odd kid but at least he was friendly. "So, what's there to do around here?" Chris asked.

"There's table tennis in the community center," Amita said, coming over to him. "And a few video games." Chris couldn't tell if she had a British accent or if she was just one of those people who liked sounding British.

Ben rolled his eyes and threw his feet up on the table, "Why would I go to the community center when I've got an X-box at home . . . Oh, wait. Never mind."

"What?" Chris asked.

"Nothing, I just forget that our internet is cut because my sister Katy tried to run away. I can't play anything online anymore. It stinks," Ben moaned.

"You mean the girl in the security office? She's your sister?" Chris shook his head, thinking, of course she is. He'd already known she was Virtanen's daughter. Still, he had trouble believing she was related to this guy.

"Where did she think she was going?" Amita asked.

"Running away with this kid Troy from our school, but she didn't get far. She ran smack dab into some sort of weirdness out past the fence."

Chris sat down on the edge of the table and noticed a large envelope in front of Ben. Chris didn't sit on it, but he was close. "Hey, watch it, you savage!" Ben shouted, grabbing the small parcel away.

"What?" Chris asked jumping up.

"You almost sat on them," Ben looked at the envelope. "I almost forgot about this." He held the package close to his chest and in a low voice said, "I don't have time for video games anyway. I've got stuff to do."

"I wasn't even close to it," Chris pointed out.

"What's in there anyway?"

Ben looked over his shoulder at the door, then said, "I've got a friend who works at the generator plant. His family is from around here. I'm going to trade this for information. . ." He looked in the envelope, then looked up at Chris and Amita, "or at least I'm going to 'loan' them for information."

He opened the envelope again and looked inside. Then he stared at Chris and Amita. "So do you guys want to find out what's really going on around here?"

"What do you mean?" Chris asked.

"He means the explosion at the observatory," Amita said. "They had an accident up there a few nights back. My parents were there. They're the head engineers for the project, but they wouldn't say what happened. They keep saying everything is fine."

"What could explode in a telescope?" Chris asked.

"A telescope? Are you having a laugh?" Amita sneered. "My parent's last job was at the CERN supercollider in Switzerland. Their specialty is building massive engines for particle physics."

"Really?" Chris asked.

"If they were out here to build a telescope, I'd be surprised," Amita said. "They'd—"

Ben interrupted. "Well, yeah, so there's that, right? Explosions and what not." He looked up, glancing at Amita, then Chris. "But then there's the monster my sister saw the other night." His eyes went back to the envelope again as he shrugged. "It killed her friend, so that might be important."

# Chapter Six

The sun was blazing overhead, scorching the dusty earth as Ben led Amita and Chris up the dirt lane to the generator building. "I feel bad for my sister," Ben said. "She was a lot happier in San Diego, and it's my fault we're here."

Back in the trailer Amita and Chris had listened to the whole story about the attack. Ben said it'd taken all night to get the story out of Katy. "The only reason she told me anything was because she's got nobody else. Plus, I asked... like a lot. She's really scared, she doesn't think any of us should be here. Plus, she's worried about her friend. I didn't know what to tell her, but she got me thinking. I've got a friend of my own who might know more about what my sister saw."

Chris wasn't sure if he believed a word of it, especially the friend part, but he had nothing better to do so he went along. He and Amita stayed to one side of the lane, trying to find any shade along the row of trailers, while Ben walked right down the middle, talking the whole time. He shook his head. "Neither of us should even be here. I made one mistake, and my aunt decided to pack us up and send us off to the desert. The principal claimed I 'terrorized' our school. How do you like that? Such crap!"

Chris stopped. "What did you do?" he asked, worried Ben was more than just the goofball he appeared to be.

Ben kept walking, saying over his shoulder, "I made a vomit storm, but I mean, it wasn't even my vomit. I just wanted to see what would happen."

"'Vomit storm? What the hell is that?" Chris asked, staring at Ben's back.

"Just wait, you've got to hear this," Amita said, hurrying past him.

Ben finally stopped and looked back at the two of them. Chris was surprised, but it seemed like he was actually embarrassed. "Look, sometimes I have trouble controlling myself. I have an idea and I start doing stuff without thinking. It's not fun, you know."

"Hey, man, I'm not going to judge you." Chris said while thinking, that's a lie.

"Go ahead and tell him, Ben. Please," Amita said, trying to hide her smile.

"Well, it was back home, after lunch on this hot day. The AC was down in our gym. But the phys-ed teacher still wanted us to play basketball. He stuck this big fan in the door. The thing was like a helicopter. It was so loud that nobody heard this one kid, a friend of mine named Freddy, say he was sick. Freddy was kind of fat. He was even bigger than you, Chris." Ben dropped the insult so fast that Chris didn't have time to react.

"Anyway, Freddy got all sweaty and blew chunks on the gym floor. It looked like he had chocolate milk too. Poor guy, like he didn't have it tough enough already. So they sent for the janitor and he put that sawdust stuff down that absorbs the puke and smells like pine trees. The fan was pushing it around on the floor, but the janitor managed to get most of it in his bucket. I was watching the couple of pieces he missed sliding around on the floor. I was right near the fan and was sort of curious what would happen if some of that sawdust got in it. I wanted to see how far it'd go.

I'll be honest I wasn't even thinking about the vomit."

"You didn't?" Chris asked.

Amita threw her arms in the air with a flourish, "Vomit storm!" She laughed.

"I dropped the whole bucket in," Ben said.

"Why would you do that?" Chris asked.

"You know, looking back I'm not sure," Ben said.

Chris stared at him with his mouth open. Ben was kicking a rock loose from the ground. "Look, sometimes I forget my medication, okay? . . .Or sometimes it just doesn't work, and I can be kind of impulsive. It's not like I don't try. It's just sometimes I do stuff without meaning to."

Chris looked back at Amita. "He keeps things interesting. You've got to admit that," she said. "If we keep him away from pointy objects, we ought to be alright."

"Who invited you anyway? Why aren't you playing ping-pong or something?" Ben motioned for her to clear off.

"Quit it," Chris said, taking the lead. He was looking up at the generator building, hoping more than anything just to get out of the heat. After the observatory, the structure housing the facilities backup power was the largest, with massive garage doors in front and fuel tanks connected by a series of catwalks in the back.

Inside there were oversized bays for earthmovers and trucks to park in. Only a few of the machines were there now as the rest were at the observatory working on repairs. Chris looked back at the white dome and could see where the scar had been sealed up. The building sat on a rocky ridge and the earthmovers were pushing dirt to the base, building a second ridge, a mound of dirt, like a ring.

'They're afraid it's going to explode again,' Chris thought as he looked at the massive piles of soil and rock. 'They're building a barricade.'

He stepped through the garage door, not finding much relief from the heat. As he smelled the thickened air of diesel exhaust he called, "Hello?" hoping Ben would catch up.

Ben and Amita had fallen behind, arguing. "You cheated somehow. I'm taller and faster than you. That should've given me an advantage," Ben complained.

"But somehow I beat you for ten straight games," Amita answered. "It's all in the wrist." She gestured as if she had a ping-pong paddle in her hand.

"I bet I could beat him, though." Ben nodded to Chris.

Chris was about to respond when someone called from beneath a large truck. "Hey, that sounds like Ben Virtanen, the boss's kid." A man came rolling out on a mechanic's creeper, wearing dirty coveralls smeared with grease and oil. He was young looking with a big smile, his dark hair cut short in a military crew cut. "What's going on there, Ben?" he asked, getting to his feet.

"Hey, Jake, I thought I'd introduce you to my new friend here." Ben turned to Chris and explained, "Jake here is a Navajo, you know like an Indian, but not an Indian like you, Amita." He nodded towards her.

"Wow, so that just happened," Amita said, shaking her head.

"What?" Ben asked.

"You just go ahead and throw things out there, don't you, kid," Jake said.

"What?" Ben asked again.

"Native American," Chris said. "Usually you'd say Native American, though most times I'd probably try to avoid introducing somebody by their race."

"Oh," Ben said. "Sorry." He glanced back at Chris. "Speaking of which..."

"Dude, if you even ask—" Chris started to say, then he stared at Ben and gave up. "Okay, if you want to know. My dad is African American, my mom is as white as you are. Hence my brother and I look so different. We've got a bunch of genes to pick from. He got my dad's skin tone and my mother's blue eyes. I got everything else, a few freckles, a tendency to burn and curly hair that sticks up no matter what I do."

"Who'd you get your weight problem from?" Ben blurted out. "Oh, man— I'm sorry— I shouldn't have said that."

"You get beat up a lot, don't you?" Amita asked.

"No . . Well, okay, maybe a few times. But you wouldn't hit me, would you, Chris?" Chris didn't answer.

Jake laughed while wiping his hands with a rag. "So, what are you guys up to?" he asked. "And what's in that envelope?"

Ben opened it and pulled out several comic books. "These are for you, man. The first twenty issues of the Walking Dead. I told you my aunt would send them. They're worth a fortune, so be careful." He handed them over.

"This is cool," Jake said, looking down at the books. He glanced at Amita and Chris. "You guys watch the show?" They both shook their heads. "You should. It's the best, real addictive, and nasty gory too. Ben here loves it. They were running a marathon in the community center when he told me he had these. I never read them before."

"Yeah, Kirkman is awesome," Ben said. "But before you read them, can you fill my friends and me in a bit more on some of those things you were talking about the other day. You know, that end of the world stuff."

"End of the world?" Jake asked confused. He tilted his head as he remembered. "What, is this some sort of sad attempt at a bribe?" He held up the books.

Ben shrugged and looked away.

Jake shook his head. "Just go look it up, kid. If you want to know about Monster Slayer and the alien gods, it's not a secret, it's all over the internet. Hell, the History channel made it seem like my ancestors were worshipping little green men." Jake's smile went away as he handed the books back to Ben. "I'm not the guy for storytelling. I'm a bad enough boy for working here with you Bilagaana."

"Actually, I can't look it up. The security creep disconnected us. My sister tried running away the other night, but then her ride was attacked by something out past the fence."

Jake was bending down and picking a wrench up off the ground. "What do you mean?"

"Alien Gods, you said they used to stalk people. Kill them, right? I think she saw one."

"Kid, the Alien Gods were massive, their bones litter the land." Jake walked to the garage door and pointed at the cliffs in the distance. "You think all these mountains are just rock, but you don't see the battles fought here." Jake paused, going back to pick up more of his tools. "That is, if you buy that sort of thing."

Jake turned to Chris and Amita. "'He listens, but he doesn't hear.' My granduncle used to say that about me too." He pointed to Ben adding, "The explosion was four nights ago, after that me and Ben were talking. I told him how we Navajo believe in a state of balance in the world. When things get out of whack, bad stuff happens. One of our founding stories was about these monsters formed when there was strife between man and woman. It was in the world before this one, but the monsters came through, here into the fourth world."

He turned and faced the dome. "I don't know what they do up there in that observatory, but they got doors on it that never open, and they're bringing in enough power to run a small city. You go near it, and you'll feel it. It vibrates right through you."

He turned back to the trio, "I'm probably one of the least spiritual Navajos you'll ever meet, but even I know something is wrong. Those monsters in the legends, people made them. From what I've seen we're still pretty good at making things to destroy ourselves."

Ben nodded. "That's what I'm saying, man. My sister was out past the fence. She saw something that sure sounds like a monster."

Jake shook his head. "It was probably a mountain lion, this is their hunting range, and they've been known to stalk people." He rubbed the side of his face, debating over saying something more.

"What?" Ben asked.

"Look, kid, I don't want to fill your head with anything else."

"Come on. We're just trying to stay safe. My dad won't tell us anything. Now you're going to start keeping secrets too? I thought you were cooler than that."

Jake looked like he was tempted to throw something at Ben. He walked towards his work bench, placed his tools down and finally said, "I got a call the morning after the explosion from my uncle. He lives a few miles from here, up towards Page. Something landed on his property. The ground was all scared up.

"He said he was going to check it out. I told him to wait for me, that I'd come out, but he said he'd be fine, didn't need me.

"He called me back later that day and said he didn't find anything, but he sounded strange. Usually, he takes the time to remind me how much he doesn't like me working here, but that night he didn't, just got off the phone real quick. I thought he was tired. Things have been a little crazy around here since that night, so I haven't gotten a chance to get out there. I really should, though."

After a while Chris, Amita, and Ben said goodbye, leaving Jake behind and headed towards the air conditioning of the community center. Amita and Chris chatted a bit, getting to know each other while Ben stayed surprisingly quiet.

## Chapter Seven

Later that night, Chris was back at his family's assigned trailer. Alex had made dinner. Earlier he'd gone to the community center where there was a small commissary. Residents could pick up groceries if they wanted to cook rather than eat in the cafeteria.

The food Alex made was healthier than most cafeteria food: lean chicken, heaps of vegetables, and a small portion of brown rice. There was enough for the whole family, but their mom was late coming home. It was well past ten. The boys waited up, playing round after round of chess, Alex's favorite game. Chris was a skilled player, but somehow, he always found a way to lose to his brother.

Chris glanced up and smiled when his mom came through the door, but the smile gave way to concern when he saw her. Strands of hair escaped a disheveled ponytail, and her ordinarily pale complexion was almost gray.

"I made some food. It's in the fridge," Alex said, his attention on the board. Chris had narrowly escaped checkmate with his last two moves, and Alex was trying to find a way to close off his escape.

"Thanks, Alex, but I think I might just go to bed. It's going to be a long day tomorrow, and for the foreseeable future. Doctor Virtanen is going to be keeping me very busy," their mom said.

Alex moved a bishop forward, then glanced at her.

"I may have to be out here longer than I thought," she said, pouring herself a glass of water from a pitcher in the fridge.

"What do you mean?" Alex asked with a tone creeping into his voice.

She came over with the glass and sat down. "Dr. Virtanen is a very driven man, sometimes too driven." She drank the water while picking up her phone and setting the alarm.

Chris's eyes were on his brother, afraid of what his mom was going to say, but more afraid of how Alex would react. His mom took a moment considering her words. "Dr. Virtanen has created something here, something potentially dangerous." She stopped and shook her head. "What am I saying? It's incredibly dangerous. I don't know what he was thinking. He's reached too far." She paused, seeing Chris's mouth begin to open. He wanted to ask her what she was talking about, but his mom shook her head as she continued. "I've got a few ideas on how to help, but it's going to take time to create what I need, and more time to test my theories. But just leaving this out here, not being part of the solution, I can't do that."

Chris wanted to blurt out, what is it? But he knew the answer he'd get.

Alex's question was less friendly. "So how long?" he demanded as he pushed back from the table.

"The data I need to go through is enough to fill a career. . . I'm sorry, but I'm going to have to be here for a while."

"You're making this sound permanent. What about Dad? What about school? What about our life back in Norfolk?"

"Alex, your dad is deployed, I don't know for how long. He could be anywhere. Look, just give me some time. This was the first day, and if you only knew, you'd understand how overwhelming it is. If it goes too long, I'll make arrangements to get you back for the school year, but right now you guys have to hang in here with me."

Alex looked like he was about to protest, but then his mom asked, "Can you be a good soldier?" His dad had been saying this to him since he was small, ever since he became an older brother. At one time he would have responded with a salute, but all he did this time was nod while his face stayed rigid with emotion. Their mom made her way back to her bedroom while Alex's hand went to his king. He laid it down on its side. "I think that's enough for tonight," he said to Chris.

Hours later Chris was lying in bed, eyes open, staring at the ceiling, listening to the air conditioner outside the window. It was humming loudly, but there was another sound, an angry throbbing in his ear. 'Some nasty creatures must be living under the trailer,' he thought. It sounded like one of those cicada bugs, but worse. The sound had more of an echo, a deeper resonance that he could feel. They had big bugs in Virginia, but nothing that could make a noise like that.

It was bright in their room with the security lights shining from the fences. Chris wasn't sure if he'd already slept or if he'd been awake the whole night. His head was running and wouldn't leave him alone. 'What's going on here?' He couldn't help thinking about it, he'd heard and seen too much not to. But along with that thought was a more familiar one. 'Where's Dad?'

Anytime his father was 'deployed,' he worried he might not come home. Chris shook his head. His father didn't have a safe job. He'd been a Navy Seal for years, but now he was officially retired, only not really. Chris's dad did 'consultant work,' for the government, the kind of stuff you didn't ask about and that he didn't talk about. When he was gone for long stretches, their mom and the boys still referred to him as being 'deployed,' but that was more out of habit.

The buzzing hadn't stopped. It was twisting in the night. 'Was it one creature or a whole swarm?' He tried pulling his pillow over his head to block the sound, but it didn't work.

He looked over at his brother, who was breathing slowly and regularly. He wondered if someday Alex's life would be the same as his father's. 'Would he have a family somewhere, worried about where he was? Would he be incredibly comfortable with a weapon in his hand?'

Chris shivered a little. It was a strange thing, knowing what your father was capable of. Like every son, he wanted to be like his dad, but that life wasn't for him. Chris didn't have it in him, not like Alex. He looked at his brother's sleeping form, watching his chest rise and fall. Then his eyes went to the window, to those glaring security lights.

There was a thump near the floor. Something smacked into the bottom of the trailer. The buzzing stopped suddenly. Now there was only the sound of the air conditioning. Throwing his blanket aside, Chris sat up, staring at the spot. He listened, waiting, suddenly aware of how thin the trailer's floor was. The buzzing started again.

Whatever made that noise was large, Chris was certain. He could feel the buzz in his feet as it started to move again.

It slipped out from under him, moving to the door, going towards the living room and kitchen, heading for the other side of the trailer where his mother's room was. Chris stayed sitting. More bumping and thumping came from the other side of the trailer. It sounded like someone was moving around.

Getting out of bed and going to the door, Chris listened. There was a weak banging in the distance. He opened his bedroom door and went into the main room, looking across at his mother's door.

There wasn't a single light on, but the living room seemed too bright. He looked towards the large windows opposite the front door with heavy curtains covering them. Light was seeping through and shining beneath the cloth

From his mother's room, he heard a jiggling knob. Someone was trying to get out. 'Was she on the other side, struggling with it?' Chris had never known her to sleepwalk. Listening carefully, he tiptoed slowly forward, past the living room, then across the front entrance.

Just before the kitchen table, he glanced at the window and saw something very bright moving out there.

He'd never seen the security lights rotate or change directions. They were fixed, but it seemed like they were dancing, glowing around the edge of the curtains, but it wasn't with the bluish glow of the powerful LEDs.

Chris thought about Ben's story as he went towards the window, feeling the buzzing again under his bare feet. He pulled back the curtains. In the distance, the lights on the fence were shining, same as ever, but below, towards the ground, just out of view, something else was glimmering.

He was tempted to open the window and stick his head out, but then he thought of that thump. He'd felt it through the floor. Ben's story about what happened to his sister and her friend continued to play in his head.

As he glanced at his mother's door, he felt something close to panic. A moment passed without any more sounds. Then he felt the buzzing move again, felt it glide away. He looked out the window and saw something fly off. Something shining with shades of pink and purple as it stayed low to the ground diving under the trailers. In a moment it was gone.

Searching his memory for every word of Ben's story, Chris felt a strange tingling along his spine as he watched the thing, knowing somehow that it was wrong. That it didn't belong here. 'Ben talks so much,' Chris thought, but he remembered the main points, the story of the lights. He wished someone else were awake, that anyone had been here to see this thing.

●

# Chapter Eight

Chris went to his mother's door, quietly turning the knob, sticking his head in. He could see her tangled up in her blankets, breathing slowly.

Glad she was safe, he nodded, then closed the door carefully before starting back to his room, knowing he wasn't going to be able to sleep. A moment before sitting down on his bed, he heard another sound. A sharp ping hit the glass of his window.

He'd had enough. He threw the curtains open, looking out just as another rock hit the glass. Ben was standing in the lane.

Chris slid the window open and whispered in a sharp voice, "What are you doing? It's four in the morning."

"It's closer to five, perfect time for a walk," Ben answered in a low voice.

Chris stared at him in confusion.

"I know where Jake's uncle lives. He's got the only piece of private land for miles around here. It'll only take a few hours to hike there." He held up a twelve-ounce bottle. "See, I even packed water."

"You're out of your mind," Chris said.

"Come on. You have to want to know what landed out there... I'm going with or without you."

Chris thought about what his mother had said. 'Dr. Virtanen has created something here, something potentially dangerous. What am I saying? It's incredibly dangerous.'

'If there was something out in the desert, it wasn't the thing she was scared of. It was whatever was in that dome that worried her. But maybe what Jake's uncle saw could give them some answers. They might even be helping his mom if they found something out there.'

Chris tensed up, feeling like it was someone else who said, "Hang on, I'll be right out." He closed the window quietly.

"What are you doing?" his brother asked from across the room.

Chris jumped a little, unable to answer.

"He tossed three rocks by the time you came in. He's lucky he didn't break the damn window," Alex said in the dark.

"He wants to go for a hike. We won't be gone long."

"A hike? That's garbage, but whatever. Just stay out of trouble," Alex said as he sat up, putting his feet on the floor.

"What are you doing?" Chris asked.

Alex stretched one arm, then the other, twisting his neck to loosen it. "Jogging again. There's not much else to do around here."

"You could try sleeping in," Chris pointed out.

"You ever see Dad sleep in?"

"No, but then again, I wouldn't have been awake for it."

"Well, there you go," Alex said as he got up and flipped on the light.

Chris got dressed and went outside to where Ben was kicking the ground impatiently. "Man, it's about time. What took you so long?" he asked. He opened the bottle of water he'd brought for the hike and drank most of it down.

Chris shook his head, glad that he'd brought another bottle for himself.

∞

Across the facility at the Patel's house, Amita's eyes popped open. She had no idea what woke her, but she wasn't happy. She didn't like it when things bothered her sleep.

Amita wasn't a deep sleeper, never had been. Sometimes she'd get tired, but sleep wouldn't come. When it finally did, anything that bothered her had a good chance of getting bludgeoned.

Reading usually helped, unless she became too engrossed in her book. Since she'd been there, she'd reread Anna Karina, the Lord of Rings trilogy and all the Sherlock Holmes mysteries, along with a number of Agatha Christi's books. That was her light reading. She'd picked some of Feynman's books about physics from her dad's shelf, but found they were less interesting than the books on forensic science she was into now. She'd been consuming them since the first attack a few days ago. Her tablet lay on her nightstand, open to a book about examining corpses.

Not everyone knew that someone else, besides Katy's friend, had been hurt. It wasn't something Doctor Virtanen wanted to be common knowledge, but Amita suspected something was up. Once she heard about what happened to Ben's sister, she formed the theory that there'd been another attack the night after the incident, after the new security head assumed control.

After Pacheco's arrival, Amita had heard her father mention that one of the lab techs was going to be disappointed that he couldn't go for hikes in the evening anymore. No one was supposed to be outside the fence without permission from the security head.

But in the morning, she'd seen men out there climbing around on the hills near one of the trails that led to the facility. It wasn't long, only a few hours afterward, that a new doctor arrived.

The medical clinic's entrance was on the opposite side of the community center from the cafeteria. Until then, it'd been little more than a glorified nurse's office, busy handing out Band-Aids and aspirin, but by the afternoon she'd seen men clearing out storage rooms to expand the space. There was security at the door, and the shades were left closed. The level of tension for everyone, which had been high enough since the explosion, ratcheted up a few more degrees.

It all added to something bad happening.

'Now they have two bodies to examine,' Amita thought as she lay in bed, still wondering why she was awake. She glanced at the window. From the second floor she had a view of almost the entire facility. That's how she knew something was moving out there. Something was shining in the dark. It reflected off the ceiling of her room.

Her house was prefabricated, built in a factory somewhere, loaded on a trailer and delivered. There were eight houses at the facility built this way, set up in a little circle, made to look like a regular suburban neighborhood. They even had driveways and mailboxes.

Amita climbed out of bed, noticing the way light twisted down below her windowsill. Pulling back the curtains she found nothing there. Whatever it was, was gone. When she looked towards the trailers, she saw the glow near the ground, half hidden by them. It went out past the fence, disappearing over the edge of the Mesa.

She thought of Ben's story and looked at his house, two driveways over. His door was opening. He stepped out and closed it carefully, looking around to make certain no one saw him. Amita watched him start toward the trailers. Saw him following in the direction the light had gone.

Quickly she got dressed and came down the stairs, going out into the road. Ben was heading down the lane, trying to be quiet and secretive, which only made him easier to follow. Amita stayed to the shadows. She had her suspicions about what he was up to, and while she didn't think it was a good idea, she didn't want him to stop either. Jake's story had piqued her curiosity.

From a hiding spot around a corner, Amita watched Ben throw a rock at the window of one of the trailers. He tapped his foot for a moment, then threw another, followed by one more. The window opened and Chris stuck his head out. A few minutes later he was outside too.

The boys started off and Amita fell in behind them, this time being even quieter. She wasn't sure if Chris would be as easy to stalk, he seemed a bit smarter than Ben. 'Well, maybe not smarter, just more observant,' Amita thought.

She followed them out to an area that was full of storage containers. A dozen lined the fence. Ben ducked between two, following a narrow corridor. Amita stayed back, watching them until they were gone. When she slowly approached, she found the boys had disappeared, but she could hear them. Ben was chattering away, talking about the opening they'd just come through.

The containers nearly touched the fence. There was no obvious opening in it, but when she moved the chain links, she noticed a place at the closest pole where a flap had broken loose.

It was easy to fold the small section back and slip through. She thought of calling out to them, but she could picture Ben giving her a hard time or Chris insisting they turn around. So, she stayed quiet, following the boys onto a narrow desert trail, trying to stay close without being noticed, aware for the first time that she had every intention of going with them to meet Jake's uncle, of seeing what, if anything, had landed there. She looked up at the early morning stars and smiled, happy to be on the trail of something.

## Chapter Nine

Alex tied his sneakers and watched his brother leave. He wasn't sure about this Ben kid. He was disruptive and out of control, barely able to sit still, all the things that Alex wasn't. He smiled a little as he thought about the kid's eyebrows and shook his head.

Alex may not have liked him, but he was glad to see Chris hanging out with someone instead of being his antisocial self. Usually, Chris didn't look up from his books long enough to talk to people. It wasn't that Alex didn't appreciate reading. He liked to read as well, but he worried his little brother did nothing else, that he spent too much time in fiction and not enough in the real world.

Alex went towards the door, glancing at his mother's room. He knew he was complaining too much, but it was hard not to be mad. He had so many things going on back in Norfolk; ROTC, sports, volunteer work, anything and everything to make him look good to the Naval Academy. This was the year for him to apply, up against thousands of applicants. It was a lot of pressure.

Stepping out the door he started running, heading down the lane, letting the first mile go by, taking an easy pace, easy for him anyway. In just under seven minutes, he covered the distance to the guard shack, about halfway to the front fence. Alex looked down at his watch before really stepping on the gas. Sixty seconds counted down while he pounded as hard as he could, having no idea how far he was going, only picking a point ahead of him to push for. His gut tightened as the seconds counted by and his heart rate increased. Alex turned and looked at the observatory, watching it move past the night sky while his arms swung up and down pumping hard.

The stars above were beginning to fade with the morning light, 'magic time,' Alex thought, remembering what his dad called it when the sun was nowhere in sight and the light faded into existence ahead of the day.

Alex pushed for a moment more, till his body was done and the time ran out. He slowed his pace going behind some larger two-story homes. The fence ran behind them. Past it was a sheer rock wall. In the daylight, the cliffs glowed in shades of red and brown, rising above the mesa. Only the observatory was taller, but not by much.

He followed close along the fence line as it climbed up a ridge that cut down from the rocks, pointing like an arrow with the observatory at its tip.

Alex looked down towards the long community center with its row upon row of trailers parked around it. Theirs was indistinguishable from the others, split into paired columns of five with lanes between them.

He came down the ridge running behind the tanks of diesel fuel at the generator building, trying to avoid breathing in the powerful fumes. On the other side, he could feel the hum of high-power lines over his head. They entered the generator building, coming in from the east, out of Page.

The ground sloped gently down towards a storage area where containers lined the fence. Alex had no idea his brother had been here only a little while before.

Looking down and away he could see the edge of the mesa where the ground dropped into a valley covered in early morning haze that was ready to fill with color. Mountains were in the distance, and although Alex didn't know their names, he was certain they were sacred to someone.

He slowed his pace, wondering if he wanted to wait for the sunrise or if he had enough time to make another lap. Dropping to a walk, he breathed in the cool morning air and enjoyed the quiet. His eyes stayed on the distant mountains, and he felt peaceful as his heartrate slackened.

Thinking about his mom, he knew he had to apologize for the way he acted last night. He didn't like the idea of her staying here, but if she felt it was important, he had to respect that. 'Maybe it'll get dad to return from wherever he is.' Alex thought about the last conversation he had with his father. They'd talked about his future, about what Alex wanted. His dad had tried again to talk him out of following in his footsteps. He was fine with his son going in the military, but he didn't love the idea of him pursuing Special Forces.

"You've got years to decide, don't close yourself off to the idea of doing something else," his father had said.

Alex had nodded in agreement, but his father knew what his son was thinking, and nothing would dissuade him. Alex was wondering what his dad was doing now when something distracted him. A light caught his attention. It was down where the fence disappeared behind the containers. A few yards past the drop-off, there was a glowing thing, and it was moving.

'Someone must be out there with an LED flashlight,' Alex thought, 'a really bright one, security probably.' But as he watched the movement, he realized the light wasn't only out past the fence, but over the edge of the cliff, floating in the air next to it, darting back and forth, too fast to be a person.

Alex started towards the containers. He lost track of the light. The huge metal boxes blocked it out. They were larger up close.

The glow from the security light couldn't penetrate the spaces between the containers. The large metal boxes were laid out in straight lines, but some were staggered, creating a dark maze where the echo of his footsteps bounced from the metal combining with a buzzing in the distance.

He passed two rows before he saw the light again. The chain links were little more than black lines against the sharp glow. The buzzing became louder as he approached.

He walked down the corridor and felt a tingle in his spine. Again, he was thinking of his mom and how worried she was about what Virtanen had made here. 'Did this have something to do with it?' She couldn't talk about her research, but Alex knew she was a physicist who did classified work for the government. 'If something scared her, then it had to be bad.'

Alex had the strangest feeling he wasn't alone as he approached the end of the container. He touched the fence and saw the light disappear, heading north.

It fell from the sky, dropping below the cliff.

Alex followed it. There was a small alley, three feet wide that had been left clear between the fence and the containers. Alex stopped once before coming out, before leaving the containers behind, pressing his face against the chain links, trying to look down, hoping to see what it was. He could hear the buzzing. Then he heard something else, footsteps not far from him.

He turned his head and saw someone climbing up a rocky ledge that jutted up from the sandy soil. It wasn't far from the path he'd run, heading back toward the observatory. From behind, Alex could see the uniform of a security officer wearing a large duty belt.

"Hey, did you see that?" Alex called as he came out into the open.

The man didn't answer. He kept walking, heading up the stone ridge. Still hearing the buzz, Alex looked back over his shoulder at the drop off, but whatever was making the noise stayed hidden for the moment.

Then suddenly, it came flying up and out, shooting over the fence right at the security officer. It was a streak of color, moving so fast that Alex couldn't make out a single detail.

The glow rested just above the guard for a heartbeat before whizzing away, going ahead of the man, low over the ridge. The rocky outcropping that the man was trying to climb blocked the view of the light.

Alex ran after it. "Hey, are you alright? You must've seen that!" he called.

The security guard still didn't speak. He'd reached the steepest part of the ridge, a section that would be tough to climb in the daylight. He was struggling, trying to go up it, climbing and falling, before finally giving up and moving across the rock wall.

Alex stopped where he was and watched the guard stumble on the rough terrain. There was something wrong with the way he was moving, like a sleepwalker.

Hearing the guard grunting as he struggled forward, Alex glanced at the man's duty belt. He was armed with a can of mace and a Glock. The last thing he wanted was to startle him. "Hey, what's going on? Are you feeling alright?" Alex approached with his hands up.

The security guard paid no attention. Alex was just about to come around and get in front of him when a sound came from the containers. He felt the noise move through the night, a metallic thunk, followed by the sound of something substantial hitting the sandy soil.

Alex looked back. A shadowy form was coming towards him with heavy footsteps. The outline of a man stood out against the dark, but Alex couldn't make out any details.

"You shouldn't be here, boy," the shadow said. Its voice was strange, inhuman, almost electronic, and filled with reverb.

Alex's whole body tightened with fear as he turned to face this new arrival. The voice was cold and sinister, but all he could see was a silhouette, an inky shape between him and the containers. Alex's eyes were used to the dark and the sunrise was on its way, so he should've been able to see more, but it was as if this person was wrapped in blackness.

"Who's there?" Alex asked.

That's when the shadowy outline began to change. The silhouette went from human to something else, something horrible. Arms grew and lengthened, twisting out into sharp points before curving back. Its shoulders spread and widened, doubling in size and its neck lengthened, while its head split in half from the chin up. Something dangled out where the man's mouth would've been, coiling like a snake.

In shock Alex watched, unable to move, unable to do anything. The shadow's legs snapped with a cracking sound as its knees popped back at an unnatural angle, like massive springs preparing to release.

It motioned towards the stumbling guard with the sharp blades that came from below its grotesquely long fingers. "He was sleeping. This isn't a good place for that." Then the shadow's feet, which had elongated, pressed down. It bounded into the air, flying over

Alex, who ducked to the side, getting out of the way while the creature landed on its target.

Its full weight smashed the security guard to the ground, flattening him on his stomach. Then its head rose, and its tongue darted out to stab the man in the neck. There was a crunch and a squish as the guard's flesh was violated.

Alex watched the whole thing while backing away. His mind was rushing. He'd seen the speed of the creature. He wouldn't be able to make it down the ridge before it had him. He wondered if he could lose the monster in the containers. 'No, it was too fast.'

Running wasn't an option.

There was no way to escape if it wanted to do to him what it'd done to the guard.

The voice spoke again as the thing rose from the guard's body. "Now, what to do with you, boy? I've got work here, and you could cause me trouble, but you could also be one of the important ones. One of the ones I'm not supposed to hurt."

Alex watched it step away from the fallen man. It coiled down as it walked. "What would you tell people? What did you see? Important or not I'm afraid you must sleep."

It leapt at him, springing forward.

The creature was quick, but Alex knew it was coming. He'd just seen it pounce. Now it was attacking the same way. This was his only advantage.

It saw a teenage boy, but the creature didn't know about the hours Alex spent in a dojo training, or the years on wrestling mats winning matches and state championships. Alex may not have been as fast as the creature, or as large, but he understood momentum.

Reaching out, Alex grasped the creature as it pounced. His hands landed on tough flesh and clenched tight, then he twisted, throwing himself around, using the creature's own speed to sling it back into the rocks. It smashed into the ground with a heavy smack while its voice squelched in anger.

Alex didn't wait for it to attack again. He dove towards the guard, reaching without looking for the man's belt. His hand strayed across the firearm, which was the obvious choice, but there was a hitch on the holster and a safety on the handgun. By the time Alex got it up to shoot, the creature would be on him. The only tactic left was calling for help.

He squeezed the security guard's radio and heard the channel open. "Attention, I need help, near the containers, northeast corner of the fence!" Alex looked up to where he'd tossed the creature, expecting a second strike, expecting to be hit, but that didn't happen. The creature wasn't there.

'Was it gone?' Alex fumbled for the gun as his eyes darted around, scanning the ridge. He expected the thing to swoop down on him. 'I need to get out of here,' he thought, pulling the gun out. As he started to move, he noticed a strange feeling.

He reached down to touch the tickling on his stomach. His hand came away wet, but there was no pain. The whole area was numb. He looked at his hand. It was hard to tell in the dark what the sticky substance was but the smell of blood was familiar. Alex thought back to the moment when the creature attacked, thought about that half second of contact.

'The creature's long arms, the way they'd hooked back, they were blades,' Alex realized.

The morning seemed to be getting darker as he looked over his shoulder at the sun coming up over the mountains. He could hear someone squawking on the radio while sleepiness overcame him. Alex didn't notice his eyes shut and he barely felt himself slump into the dirt.

# Chapter Ten

The sun started to rise, and already Chris could tell it was going to be a hot day. 'Big surprise in the desert,' he thought as he stared down at the dirt trail. He called to Ben, "You sure this is the way? It's not much of a road."

"Jake's uncle's place is the only private property around here for miles. The rest is nationally protected park land."

"So how far is it?" Chris glanced back over his shoulder at the facility, but the rocky cliffs covered it from view. He wasn't looking forward to the hike back. To the right was a valley spreading out forever and a desolate highway running down the middle. Only a single truck had gone down it in the last hour and it'd been so far away it looked more like a fast-moving insect.

"A few miles. Should only take us an hour or so," Ben said.

Chris looked ahead at the trail. At first, it seemed to be heading towards the valley floor, but then it leveled off, traveling back up along the rocky ledge, circling the mesa towards the north. The ground turned red as the sun climbed higher. "We've already been gone for over an hour," he said.

"Yeah so, we'll just walk faster."

"Maybe we could just jog," Chris scoffed.

Ben looked Chris up and down, his face saying everything.

"I wasn't serious— and, you know I can actually run pretty fast."

"Downhill maybe," Ben said dismissively.

Chris stopped walking and balled his fists. He wasn't a violent kid, but he really wanted to smack Ben in the back of the head. Luckily, Ben kept going, getting further away, not even thinking about what he said. Chris took a deep breath and let it out.

"What we should've done is hotwire that pickup back there," Ben said over his shoulder. Up ahead the road took a sharp turn, he kept walking till he was almost out of Chris's sight around the corner. When Ben realized he was alone, he came back a little and demanded, "What?"

"First off, you don't know how to hotwire a car, and neither do I, and secondly, I've had enough of your comments about my weight." Chris shook his head. "This is nuts anyway. I'm heading back." He turned and started walking.

"What? Why?" Ben called behind him, taking a moment to glance over the edge of the road before following him and calling, "Hey man. I'm sorry, really."

Chris was tempted to start running and leave Ben behind, but he didn't want to exhaust himself in the heat. Looking up the trail and at the rocky cliff face next to it, he searched the horizon for any sign of the facility, but the white dome wasn't in sight.

He did see something though, and it made him stop in his tracks. There was movement. A trail of debris falling from behind a pile of boulders. Dust and rock tumbled onto the dirt road. Chris realized they weren't alone. Someone or something was back there.

Chris listened harder as his eyes searched for any sign of what it was. Of course, it was tough hearing anything with Ben still shouting behind him. "Come on, man! I'm going with or without you. If I don't

make it back, it's totally going to be your fault for abandoning me."

"Knock it off!" Chris shot at him. He was leaning down, looking for anything he could use to defend himself with, remembering what Jake had said about mountain lions stalking people. He had no idea what had attacked Katy the other night, but he'd seen that weird light from the trailer. Then, this morning they found the pick-up truck abandoned on the road. It was enough to assure him that something bad had happened out here.

Ben was quiet only for a moment, then he called again, "What is it? What do you see?"

Chris bent down and found a large rock. He hefted it with both hands, lifting it over his head before slowly approaching the cliff wall. He could hear something moving back there behind the boulders. As more dirt slipped down onto the trail, he came around the corner with his rock in the air, ready to throw it, to smash whatever was hiding.

He nearly slipped and dropped it on his foot when he saw Amita's large green eyes staring up at him.

She held up her hands. "Well, you caught me."

Chris was too surprised to say anything. Ben came running up next to him and asked, "What's she doing here?"

Chris carefully placed the heavy rock on the ground. "How should I know? Obviously, she followed us." He offered his hand to Amita, helping her to her feet. "How long have you been on our trail?"

"Pretty much the whole time. I saw Ben leave his house and I followed him to your place. When you guys went through the fence, I had a pretty good idea where you were heading." She dusted herself off, then added, "By the way, it's not that hard to hotwire a car, especially an old truck like that one. I could get it running in no time."

"How do you know how to hotwire a car? You can't even drive." Ben asked.

Amita bit her lip, debating over whether she wanted to answer. She'd been accused of bragging before. Finally, she said, "A few summers back, while we were in Switzerland, my dad and I built a remote control car from scratch. I did all the wiring myself." "So, that's not that big a deal," Ben said.

"It was an actual car, like one big enough to carry people. I'm pretty sure I could connect a few wires and energize the starter on an old piece of junk like that." She pointed back up the trail.

"We're not doing that," Chris said.

"Why not. I want to see her try."

"No. One, that might be considered grand theft auto, and two, none of us should be driving on these narrow-as-hell trails when we don't have licenses, and three, now that Amita is with us, we definitely need to head back. Her parents are going to freak out when they realize she's gone," Chris said, looking back up the trail.

"But we're almost there." Ben was moving towards the bend in the road as he spoke.

Chris shook his head. "You don't even know where the ranch is."

"Yes, I do." Ben pointed towards the ledge. "I was going to tell you. It's just over here in the valley. I saw it."

Chris turned to Amita, hoping she'd understand, that she'd be reasonable, but she was already moving towards Ben. "We've already come this far," she said as they started walking again.

Chris went over to the ledge and looked down. 'This is nuts,' he thought, then ran to catch up with the others.

∞

While her brother was out hiking into the desert, Katy was sitting on the edge of her bed trying to decide what to do. She didn't see the point of going to class. She'd skipped yesterday, despite her dad making it very clear that he wanted her to meet the new kids. Given that the attack had been the night before, it was understandable that she was feeling anti-social.

Today was a new day and while Katy had no interest in listening to the teacher her father had hired, she could be talked into going, if for no other reason than to warn these new arrivals.

Amita would be there too. Katy liked her, and Amita seemed to feel the same, but they were more than three years apart in age. Katy would be graduating next year, while Amita, if she were anyone else, wouldn't have started high school yet.

Amita had never been in a regular school. The programs she'd gone through in London and Switzerland were for genius level kids, supplemented by tutors in places like this facility. Katy found Amita's intelligence intimidating. Sure, Katy's dad was a brilliant physicist, but she'd never had much luck talking to him.

It wasn't that Katy didn't do well in school. She was on the honor roll and took AP classes, but Amita was on a whole other level, an actual genius. It was kind of scary talking to her. Katy spent most of the time worrying that the younger girl was judging her for not being quick enough.

Still, she wanted to talk to someone about the other night. Pacheco and her father had warned her not to. She'd already ignored them. It wasn't a secret anymore after telling Ben. Now she wanted to know what Amita thought. 'The little genius might be able to shed some light on what happened.' Katy looked at the sketches she'd done of the creature. They were dark and useless, but she packed them and started getting dressed.

She was in her closet with the bedroom door half open when she heard her father's voice answer phone.

'Well, at least he made it home last night, she thought.'

The tension in his voice echoed up the stairs. "Wait, what? Inside the grounds?" There was a pause then she heard him ask, "Who was it?"

Katy crept toward the door. "There were two? Oh no, do not tell me that. Not one of the boys. Why was he out so early? . . . No, I'll tell Ellen. It should come from me. . . What do you mean, different how? Will he be alright? Fine, I will meet you at the med center in five minutes."

Katy heard her father gathering his things, his keys jingling as he took them off the hook. Her hand tightened on the door. She thought of her friend waiting in the med center and of the way she'd been interrogated. Throwing the door open, she stormed down the stairs. "It's happened again, didn't it?" she demanded.

Her father was almost outside. He turned to look at her. "I haven't time for this now."

"I warned you, I told you it wasn't safe," she said coldly.

61

Dr. Virtanen ran his hand back through his hair, staring at the floor. "Keep an eye on your brother and stay in today, okay?"

"But Dad—"

"Just do it, Katy!" he shouted, slamming the door behind him. Katy wanted to yell after him. Instead, she looked at her brother's room. 'He wasn't up yet, which was odd,' she thought.

# Chapter Eleven

It'd been over an hour since Ben spotted the ranch. The dirt road along the mesa had forked off, going down into the valley, heading toward a flat little home surrounded by corrals, sheds, and barns. As they came closer, the pinion trees and scrub brush gave way to dry grass. In the distance was a row of slowly spinning windmills.

'They'd been gone too long,' Chris thought. 'By now class had started and people were probably looking for them.'

The trio passed a small, round structure made of mud and wood that sat back from the trail. A woven blanket hung in its doorway. Amita and Chris looked at it curiously while Ben continued towards the main house. Not a pretty home, its ancient paneling was worn by the sun to a dull gray and the roof was sagging onto a farmer's porch that circled it.

Ben knocked on the screen door. The sound echoed on the aluminum as he called, "Hello, hello. Is anyone home?" He pulled the screen open and reached for the knob.

"What are you doing?" Chris asked, placing his hand on Ben's arm.

"I'm going to stick my head in and see if he's home."

"You don't just stick your head into someone's house."

"Jake said his uncle sounded weird. I think checking on him is the right thing to do. I mean what if the guy was attacked? He could be lying dead in the middle of the floor or something."

"Ooh, let's see!" Amita sounded a little too excited as she pushed past the boys and tried the door herself. It wouldn't budge. Disappointed she stepped back. "I wouldn't think someone who lived out here, where it's so isolated, would worry about locking their door."

Ben grabbed a plastic lawn chair from the front step and started going around the house looking in windows. The glass was dirty and sandblasted, but the curtains were open, giving him a clear view of the inside.

Chris followed him. "That's not cool. He's probably still sleeping. He's going wake up to your face staring at him."

"That'd scare anyone," Amita added.

"Hey, this is a public service. He could be hurt. Besides, I don't think he's home. It looks pretty empty in there."

Chris and Amita followed Ben as he went from window to window till they were in the back by the corrals. There were two barns and a number of sheds along with a chicken coop full of dirty birds pecking at the ground.

"Look at this goofball," Ben said, pointing to a goat up on top of one of the sheds. It was staring down at them and its gaze was full of distrust. The horses didn't even look up, ignoring them altogether.

"I bet he's in there," Amita said as she pointed back towards one of the barns. An empty corral surrounded it. The horses were across the way, kept in by a simple post and beam fence, but this corral was made of wire, surrounded by a second fence. The barn doors were open, but the inside was dark with only a few beams of sunlight streaming in through loose boards.

64

The trio came close to the fence, peering into the dark. Something was moving in there. "Hello," Amita called. There was no answer, but there was a snuffling sound. Something was breathing. They watched in anticipation as it came forward. It was much bigger than the horses, and there were horns on either side of its massive head. Dark brown eyes stared at them from beneath a head full of thick white hair.

"Wow, what is that thing?" Ben asked.

"I have no idea," Chris answered.

"It's a white buffalo," a voice said from the behind them. "They're very rare. I've been caring for this one since it was born."

The trio turned to see a man wearing a woven cowboy hat with a feather sticking out of it and white hair tucked beneath. Despite the heat, he wore a flannel shirt buttoned to the top. His face was aged, weathered and as solid as the rocky mesa the trio had climbed down from. Joseph Bizahalone, Jake's uncle, stared at them sternly and asked, "Who are you and why are you on my property?"

They looked at each other, trying to come up with some response. Finally, Ben stammered out, "We're looking for Jake—- I mean we're friends of Jake's. He. . . Ah, he told us something happened out here a few nights ago and. . . ."

"Well? What about it?"

"You saw something?" Chris asked.

The old man glanced towards one of his fields. When his eyes returned to the teens, he asked, "You came from that observatory, or whatever that place is, didn't you?"

They nodded their heads, except for Ben, whose attention had returned to the buffalo. "Why's it white?" he asked. The creature had come out further in the corral, sniffing the air.

"Because it was born that way," the uncle said. "I'm going to call my nephew and have him talk to your parents." Bizahalone turned, heading towards the house. "Now get away from my buffalo."

Before he could take another step, Amita grabbed the man's arm. He stopped, looking down at the hand as she asked, "You were in the Hogan, weren't you? You slept there last night?"

Though Joseph wasn't large, Amita was so small that he towered over her. He would've been able to pull away easily. "Yeah so?" he growled. He glanced at her pleading eyes and softened. "What about it?"

"The Hogan, it's for religious ceremonies, right? Something was bothering you. For some reason, you felt you had to be out there last night? What rite did you perform?"

The old man shook his head. "Kid, you think you know something, but you don't. Yeah, I slept in my Hogan last night. I sleep there all the time. And yes, something is bothering me, too much foolish company."

Amita wouldn't let go of his hand, wouldn't look away as she begged, "People are being hurt. We wouldn't have come and bothered you if we didn't think it was important."

The old man's eyes went back out to that same field. He shrugged. "I'll bring you out there and show you, but I'm still calling Jake first."

He saw the gratitude on Amita's face. "Don't get your hopes up. What you're looking for is already gone. Something dragged it away."

# Chapter Twelve

Alex opened his eyes to the sound of voices. They were distant, out in a hall, away from the room. His head felt fuzzy and when he tried to sit up, he immediately regretted it. The pain nearly overtook him, causing him to fall back and briefly black out again. The steady beep of a heart monitor sped up with his effort and slowed again as he settled back.

The voices were still talking. He looked toward a door, recognizing the gruff voice of Pacheco, the security head. "When will he be awake? I have questions I need answered," he demanded.

Alex's hand went to his stomach. That's where the pain came from. His fingers searched the bandages, touching the edges of gauze and thick trauma dressings. He was in some sort of a medical ward that was cramped with supplies stacked in every corner. IV bags, hung above his head, ran fluid into his arms. There was an opaque window on the hall where he could see the silhouette of two people.

"I couldn't tell you," the other person answered. "The toxin is so potent that it's kept the others comatose for days. The boy's different though, he doesn't have a wound on his neck, so the neurotoxin didn't permeate his blood stream. It's only on the surface and around the wound, just enough to numb him. And the blade was so sharp that I doubt he'd have felt it. Whatever is out there, it must be an amazing predator."

Alex's eyes were drifting shut. He tried to focus, but it was nearly impossible. The door opened as Pacheco corrected the other man. "It's not a predator."

"What makes you say that?" A man in a white coat followed Pacheco into the room. In the distance, there was the sound of a door opening and footsteps coming down the hall. Pacheco lowered his voice. It was only because he was so close that Alex could hear him as he said pointedly, "'Predator,' suggests that it's taking some sort of sustenance from its prey. As it's not eating them, we can't define it as such in the classical sense."

"Interesting," the doctor said.

Through half closed eyes Alex saw Pacheco turn. He was fuzzy but Alex still recognized his broad, muscular back. He saw him take the doctor by his shoulders. The footsteps in the distance were getting louder. "I need to speak to this boy as soon as he wakes up. Make certain I'm the first to know," Pacheco growled.

Alex was still trying to stay awake, but he could feel himself fading. He could also hear his mother's voice, along with Dr. Virtanen. "They're not in class, so where are they?" she demanded.

"I'm sure they're fine—-" He heard Dr. Virtanen begin, but his mother interrupted.

"You should've told me. I never would've brought my children here!" she shouted.

Alex heard Virtanen and his mom's footsteps come through the door, "I was going to tell you, but there was so much I wanted to show you first. So much work to do," Virtanen said.

"You and your work!" Alex's mom snapped.

"He hasn't woken yet, but his vital signs are strong. He's a very healthy young man," the doctor offered.

Alex felt his mom's hand touch his face. She was close to him.

"It's our work, Ellen. This is all based on your theories," Virtanen said.

Alex could almost see her, but his eyes had narrowed to slits. He struggled to open them. He wanted to say something, wanted to tell her that he was fine, but he couldn't make a sound. All he could do was listen to his mother say, "They should've stayed theories. What you've made, it's just too dangerous."

Virtanen was there by the bed. "Every great discovery comes with inherent risks. You know that. When we created—"

His mother interrupted again with her voice low. "That's what I've been trying to tell you. . ." She paused and added in a whisper that only Virtanen should've heard, "It takes two points. You think you created this thing yourself, but you may have had help from the other side."

Virtanen remained silent.

"What's that? What do you mean?" the doctor asked from the door.

Pacheco, who apparently had excellent hearing, answered. "She means that Dr. Virtanen contacted something, something that wanted very badly to come here."

It was the last thing Alex heard before fading completely into darkness.

# Chapter Thirteen

Ben, Chris, and Amita waited outside to hear what Jake's uncle had to say. Joseph Bizahalone stepped out of his house after speaking to his nephew. "You kids caused some serious trouble back there. Jake said they were in 'full disaster mode,' looking for you three. Said some 'bad stuff' has been going on." He turned and locked his door. "You sure you still want to go out there? Maybe you ought to start heading home instead?"

"We want to know what's happening and no one is going to tell us anything back there," Amita pointed out. Then she looked at the front door and asked, "Hey, how come you lock your house when there's no one around for miles?"

"Witches." Joseph answered without a hint of humor, coming down off the step. "I don't think you're going to find answers out there, but I'll show you what I saw." He walked past the trio, moving with long strides. "We've only got a little while. Jake is on his way to pick you up."

The three of them had to run to catch up as Bizahalone headed out into a field north of his house. "If you were up there the night it happened, you can imagine what I saw from here. There were those lights, coming up over the mesa," he said.

"My dad said it was an explosion in the observatory," Ben offered.

"My parents gave me that line too," Amita added.

Chris glanced back and forth between his friends in frustration. "Hey, I wasn't here yet. Mind filling me in?"

Amita nodded. "It was late at night. It woke me up, but it didn't make much noise. There wasn't a pop or

71

anything like that, just the sound of something large being torn apart. The walls of the observatory sounded like they were screaming. Then there was this light that filled the whole sky."

"It didn't look like any explosion I've ever seen," Joseph added. "I was out by the barn, checking the horses. When I looked up, I saw this glow streaming off into the sky, swallowing the stars."

"Yeah, my dad said the explosion let out some kind of gas. That what we saw was the moonlight reflected on it," Ben said. Amita and Joseph both looked at Ben as if he should've known better.

They walked out into the field, which rolled with small hills covered in rocky outcroppings. Tough looking pinion trees gave shade to small patches of grass. Coming over the rise, they saw what they were heading for, a distant pile of wreckage and smashed lumber.

Joseph pointed towards the wreckage. "After the light show something came over the mesa, right out of the brightest part of that supposed gas cloud. It shot up into the sky and came crashing down out here."

"I called Jake in the morning and waited till first light to go and see what it was. What I saw— Well, I can't really explain it."

Ben, Amita, and Chris waited for him to say more, but Joseph went silent. He continued walking, forcing the trio to jog behind him. Finally, Ben asked, "Was it one of those alien gods Jake told me about?"

Joseph stopped for a minute, turning to Ben. "My nephew told you about that?" he asked.

Ben shrugged, struggling to remember what Jake had said. "A little bit. He said they used to kill people."

Joseph nodded. "They hid by our roads, waiting to devour us. They came from the world before this one, aberrations that murdered without mercy."

"What happened to them?" Chris asked. He was still trying to figure out what the wreckage ahead of them had been. The debris field went on for some distance.

Joseph didn't break stride as he said, "Very few people were left alive. The creatures killed most everyone, but then the warrior twins were born. Their names were Slayer of Alien Gods and Born for Water. They destroyed the monsters, then only a few were left, those responsible for old age, cold, poverty and hunger."

"So, the Alien Gods were myths?" Amita asked.

Joseph looked at her. "I wasn't there so I can't say for sure. And if it makes you feel better you can call their story whatever you like. It won't change what I believe."

As they came closer to the wreckage, Chris was able to understand what had been destroyed. The fan blades of a windmill were scattered everywhere, beams that'd held it up were shattered and splintered, and parts of a water pump were buried in the sandy soil, broken and useless. Joseph went over to pick up a piece of pipe.

The windmill had sat above a well, taking ground water from deep beneath the earth. Joseph used the pipe to point. "This is all useless junk now, but the morning I came up here, I was less concerned about the damage and more interested in what had crashed." He walked along the wreckage field toward the deepest gouge.

"It must've hit the windmill on its way down, landing here and skidding." He pointed up the trail to a freshly dug embankment torn into the sandy soil.

"That's where it stopped."

"Was it a jet or something?" Ben asked.

"Not quite. That'd be easier to explain." Joseph took off his hat and looked at it, then squinted into the morning sun. "I've never seen anything like it . . . It was a jewel, like a giant diamond, nearly the size of my truck. It was beaten up a bit, but for the most part, it looked intact, which if you look at the trail it left," he pointed back, "You got to wonder how it survived."

Ben climbed down into the path cut in the ground.

The scar was deep, as if dug by an oversized plow. "Well, you said it was made of diamond. That's supposed to be pretty tough, right?" he asked.

Joseph pulled his hat down tight. "I said it looked like a diamond. It may have been closer to glass, but you couldn't see through it. In fact, everywhere it wasn't covered in dirt, it was reflective, like a mirror. It looked like steam was coming off it, but as I got closer, I realized it was mist, cold mist. It was like getting near an air conditioner."

"Like it'd been super cooled?" Amita asked.

"Yeah exactly," Joseph said. "I went to the ranch to get my truck, but when I got back it was gone. Someone had taken it."

Chris was stepping over the ton of pushed up dirt.

"What makes you so sure someone took it?" "Because I found their tracks and followed them. They led off to the slot canyons to the east. Their trail wasn't hard to follow. It looked like they dragged the thing most of the way. Occasionally they had to lift it though, when they needed to move over a rock or something. That's when their tracks got strange." Joseph stopped, his attention turning back towards home. "Looks like your ride is here," he said.

Chris and Amita glanced back at the ranch where a pick-up truck was pulling out into the field, bouncing and bumping over the rocky terrain, sending up a dust trail as it headed towards them. Joseph offered his hand down to Ben, who was struggling to get up out of the ditch. "Come on, kid. Time to face the music."

Ben took the hand, asking, "What do you mean the tracks looked strange?"

Joseph started walking back towards the truck. He said quietly, "There were two sets, one right on top the other like they belong to the same creature. They were big too, size of a buffalo or some other large animal. But they only had three toes and those toes had claws, dangerous looking. For the life of me I can't figure out how the thing was moving. Its strides were strange."

"What do you mean?" Chris asked.

The pick-up stopped nearby. Jake got out, waving them with his brow furrowed. Joseph glanced at his nephew before answering, "They were just strange. I've tracked every creature that ever crossed this desert, and these weren't like anything I'd ever seen before."

## Chapter Fourteen

Alex felt a hand on his shoulder. Someone was next to him.

"Hey, kid, can you hear me?" a voice asked.

Alex was still in darkness, unsure how long ago he'd heard his mother's voice. It could've been minutes, days or hours. There was a groaning sound. It took him a moment to realize he was the one making it.

Managing to bring one hand up to his face, he used it to rub his eyes, getting them to open as he took a sharp breath. He looked around, but everything still seemed fuzzy. He was fairly sure there was a girl standing next to him. When he tried speaking to her it came out as a dry croak.

"You guys should've never come here," she said, sounding like she was speaking to herself.

"Who are you?" he managed to grumble, but he wasn't certain the words came out. He rolled a little, trying to turn towards her and groaned with the effort and the pain coming from his abdomen.

"I'm Katy, Dr. Virtanen's daughter. I saw you and your brother when you first arrived at the security office."

Alex nodded his head, tempted to close his eyes again as tried to remember what he'd heard before he fell back to sleep. 'What had his mother said?'

Something important.

"Water?" he asked.

Katy turned, looking around and found a small plastic bottle, broke the seal and held it up to his mouth. "I'm not supposed to be in here," she said, looking over her shoulder. "But I have a friend who was attacked. My dad won't tell me anything about his condition. I'm not sure he's even alive."

A few drops spilled into Alex's mouth. The water was warm but still felt good. His hand went to his face, trying to rub the confusion away. "This thing . . . It's happened before? There were other attacks?" He got the words out in a broken whisper. Then he took the bottle from her hand.

"The others are in a different room. They look worse than you."

Alex got up onto his elbow and drank some more. The room started to spin, but he wouldn't lay back. He closed his eyes waiting for it to pass, then worked his way up to a sitting position. As he leaned forward, he felt the aching in his abdomen get worse. He focused on breathing. The pain was awful, but it was helping him focus.

"Maybe I should get the doctor?" Katy asked.

Alex shook his head. "Forget him. I don't need a doctor. Besides, he was in here earlier. I could hear him. Sounded like he was more interested in whatever did this than in helping me."

Katy nodded. "He's only been here a few days. I don't really know him, but he's kind of creepy."

"What do you mean?"

"He left my friend lying in the desert while he examined the scene of the attack. Then when he checked on me, he acted all friendly at first, but he seemed disappointed that I got away untouched."

Alex pointed to his gauze-wrapped stomach. "He probably likes me better."

"Yeah probably," Katy said.

"I saw it," Alex said. "I saw what did this . . . It looked like a man. I couldn't tell who, but it was human, then it changed." He slid down off the bed, putting his weight on his legs. They nearly crumpled under him.

Katy grabbed him to keep him from hitting the ground. "Whoa there, don't push so hard!" She wrapped her arms around his torso, holding him up.

"I want to see the others. Show me." Alex pulled away, trying to stabilize himself and step forward.

"They're this way," Katy said starting towards the doorway. She offered her hand, but he shook it off, forcing himself to walk on his own.

It was a short distance to the larger room where the victims were laid out. Inside there were three beds and three bodies. Their faces were relaxed, gray and ashen. Each one was hooked to a heart monitor beeping slowly. 'Way too slow,' Alex thought.

Katy went to the one in the middle. She hesitated for a moment, then her hand touched his cheek.

"That's your friend? Were you guys close?" Alex asked.

"We were friends, maybe more— I don't know. I mean he drove all the way out here to get me. I guess we were kind of together." She was looking down at his face. "Do you think they're going to be alright?"

"I've no idea," Alex said before tilting his head and listening. A door opened and closed. Alex looked at Katy putting a finger to his lips and coming around the table. The rip in his stomach hurt like crazy as he ducked down, but he didn't make a sound looking toward the hallway.

Footsteps passed by as someone went into the room where he'd been in. "It's time to wake up, my young friend. You have so many things to tell me," he heard the person say. The voice died. "What the—"

Alex peeked over Katy's friend and through the door. He could see the doctor staring at his empty bed. The man turned and hurried back up the hall.

"We need to get out of here," Alex whispered.

There's a back door," she offered. "I left it open."

"No, I mean we need to get out of the desert, away from this place. I need to get my mom and my brother, and we need to put some distance between us and whatever mess your father made out here. Do you know where my family is?"

For a moment Katy hesitated. "Your mom is at the observatory. Your brother. Well, he's a different story."

## Chapter Fifteen

Jake was out of his truck before the dust trail had even settled. "Come on, guys. We've got to get you home," he called, waving his arm for a moment before noticing the ground. The soft, sandy soil was thrown and buried beneath a wave of darker dirt. He closed the door of his pick-up truck and started across the field, staring at the damage.

"What happened out here?" he asked his uncle.

"Where's your windmill?"

"It's all over the place," Joseph said, staring back.

"You told me it was no big deal, not to worry. What did this?" Jake asked. The others reached him, but he'd kept going towards the destruction.

"It came from that place you work for. I saw it fly over the mesa—"

"Tell him what it was! Tell him about the tracks!" Ben interrupted.

Joseph looked down, and Ben immediately went quiet.

Jake picked up part of a windmill blade, narrowing his gaze as he examined it. "Tell me," he said to his uncle as he stepped over the gouged-up earth.

Joseph repeated his story, gave his nephew every detail of what he saw, the lights the diamond, the way it'd been dragged off. He explained a bit more about the tracks. "They were four-footed at times, then only two. One set was larger and wider than the other. I don't know what they're playing with up there, but that observatory is doing more than just observing."

Jake shook his head. "Before the explosion you would've never thought anything was wrong if I hadn't mentioned it to you. I should've never told you about all the weirdness and the power they're using." This was an old argument between them. "I had a bad feeling about it before you ever said a word, now look at this." Joseph pointed towards the ground.

"I only took the job so I could be closer to you," Jake shot back.

Joseph shrugged, turning away.

Ben was swinging his head back and forth between the two men, his mouth open, ready to butt in. He hooked his fingers in his belt loop, trying to sound very serious. "Maybe we should take a look at those tracks. What direction did you say they were heading in?"

"No way," Jake said. "I'm taking you right back to your dad. People are freaking out back there." He glanced at Chris for a moment. "You guys got everyone riled up."

Chris's brow furrowed, while Jake ignored his questioning glance. Jake didn't want to have to be the one to tell him about Alex and if he was, he'd rather it be in the truck on the way back. Chris's mouth opened ready to ask a question, but Ben wasn't done. "Look, Jake. We're already out here. Your uncle said he thought the tracks were heading for the snot canyons, I mean, how far could those be?"

"'Slot,' not 'snot,'" Joseph corrected. "And they're about three miles to the north."

Amita shook her head, "Seriously, why would anyone ever name something snot—" she started, but Ben cut her off.

"Whatever. My point is we've got a mystery. People are being hurt, and we could solve it." Ben turned to Jake. "Come on man, be someone's hero. Let's do this."

Jake was ready to say no, but Ben kept going. "Look, before you shut us down, let me make you another offer. The Walking Dead, I'll give you the books, all of them, free and clear, all yours. They're worth a ton." Ben grabbed his arm, hoping for some sign that he was getting through.

He continued, "We follow the tracks for a bit. When we get back, we can tell my dad about everything we saw. We could probably tell him right where this thing is." Jake was trying to pull his arm away, but Ben clung to it.

"It's only three miles, that's not that far. You've got to want to know. Your uncle is out here by himself. Look at him. He's frail." He pointed to Joseph. "Do you really want him unguarded and unaware?"

Joseph took his hat off and punched the inside of it. He looked like he was ready to explode at Ben.

Jake finally managed to pull his arm free. "That's enough already, I'll take you!" he yelled. "Jeez, anything to shut you up."

He started walking away, but then he turned back and stabbed his finger in Ben's chest. "This is it though, no more of this running around garbage. We follow the tracks for a bit, then you go home and stay there." Jake stormed towards his pick-up, got in and slammed the door. "Well, hurry up, all three of you," he ordered through the window.

Chris followed as Ben and Amita ran to the truck.

"This is not a good idea," he muttered.

## Chapter Sixteen

Alex and Katy slipped out the back door of medical center, into a wide hallway that ran past the cafeteria. There were double doors at either end of the hall. The ones on the right lead to the trailers where Alex could rest safely.

He went left instead.

"Where do you think you're going?" Katy asked, glancing at the cafeteria windows. There were only a few people inside having a late lunch and none looked up to see Alex struggle by.

He didn't answer, moving past the entrance to the rec center and the commissary, struggling towards the back exit. He glanced at Katy. "I'm going there." He pointed out the window at the observatory. She wanted to tell him what a bad idea that was, but Alex had already shoved the release bar, pushing the exit open. He slipped out and Katy grabbed the door before it closed all the way.

She followed Alex as he crossed forty yards of open space, dropping to his knee as he reached a dirt mound. There wasn't much cover between the community center and the base of the observatory. The only break to the landscape was the rise it sat on and the ring of earth circling around it. 'It wasn't like they were doing anything wrong,' Katy thought. 'Alex wasn't a prisoner.' It shouldn't be necessary for him to escape from the medical center, but when she thought of Pacheco and the way he'd kept her in that interrogation room, or the way the doctor had treated her friend's body like a specimen, she understood the anxiety she felt and why Alex didn't want to be spotted.

Katy looked back at the main entrance of the clinic, then towards the generator facility. It was the middle of the day, and people were all around. Before leaving the medical center, Alex had found his sneakers and running shorts, but his ripped shirt was gone so he was wearing a hospital gown. As he moved, it was flapping in the wind like a white flag. 'Yeah, that's not going to call attention at all,' Katy thought, shaking her head.

Alex held his stomach making his way to the rock wall at the observatory's base. He looked down its length. The easiest way up was the road.

Katy came up next to him. "What are you trying to do?"

"I need to get inside, get to my mom." Katy started towards the road.

"No," Alex said. "If we're seen, they'll send me right back to the medical unit. That doctor will probably drug me or something." He looked at the wall. "We have to go up here." Getting ready to climb, he controlled his breathing while the sutures holding him together stretched and the pain got worse.

Katy watched him pause, curl up and moan a little.

"Are you alright?" she asked, seeing how his skin was turning pale.

Alex nodded. "I feel like garbage, but there's something else. Look." He touched his arm and felt the hair stand up straight. A current of static electricity ran over his whole body. "This is weird."

Katy looked down at his arm, then at her own, "Yeah, I feel it too." She glanced up at the observatory filling the sky above them. "This is stupid, only authorized personnel are allowed in there. You won't make it past the door."

Alex nodded again, then stubbornly started to climb. It was six feet to the base of the observatory. Katy watched him go. For a moment she was tempted to grab his leg and pull him back down, but instead she followed.

There was a narrow strip of land at the top, running next to the observatory's pedestal. Although the whole thing was more than thirty feet tall with offices in it, there wasn't a single window, just a painfully white metal wall reflecting the sun's glow as it curved away.

They followed the curve till they came to an alcove with a set of recessed double doors. Alex tried pulling them open, but they didn't move. He pulled again, then kicked, "Come on!" he shouted.

A voice called down, clear and distant. "What are you two doing here? This area is off limits."

Katy looked around and saw a small camera.

"He's here to see his mom, Doctor Johnson. I'm Doctor Virtanen's daughter."

"I know who you are," the voice was monotone. "And this area is still off limits. Clear out and I'll let your parents know you were here."

Alex leaned against the wall, sliding towards the ground. He'd made it here on adrenaline, which was starting to fail. "Forget that. Get my mother out here now." Alex tried to shout, but his voice was weak.

Katy watched the color of his dark skin fade. "Look, he's not leaving till he talks to his mom."

Alex nodded in agreement. Then he looked at the ground as it started to spin. Katy reached out, but she was too late.

"Damn," Alex said as his legs gave up, losing all strength.

# Chapter Seventeen

Jake's truck had a bench seat wide enough for Ben, Chris, and Amita. Chris was the only one to bother looking for seat belts. The first one he found was in the middle and he pointed it out to Amita. "Thanks," she said, buckling herself in. Chris found another and started to close it. They were still out in Joseph's field bouncing over the uneven ground.

"What about me?" Ben asked, holding onto the window frame to keep from smashing his head into the dashboard. Chris shrugged just as Jake swerved a little to catch a dip in the ground, sending Ben towards the ceiling.

"Don't worry, kid. You'll be alright," Jake kept his eyes ahead of him and smiled. "We'll be on a trail soon."

"I thought you were going to follow the tracks?" Ben rubbed his head.

"My uncle said this thing went towards the canyons. There's soft soil there. He's a lot better at tracking than me, but I should still be able to find something like that. Besides driving across that much country would destroy my truck."

When they got to the trail, it wasn't much better than the open field. The ground was flatter, but it was still broken and rutted. Jake accelerated as he pulled onto it, following it for a mile, then pulled off onto a smaller trail. Within a few minutes, cliff walls began to encircle them.

Jake dropped into a lower gear as the terrain turned loose and sandy. Chris heard the truck struggle a little before Jake pumped the gas. "Are we going to get stuck down here?" Chris asked.

"No, I've got it. The sand here is extremely fine, almost like powder." Jake pointed at the cliffs. "This rock is sandstone. It's real soft. Over thousands of years rain fall runs through it, making these canyons. Even the Grand Canyon was made that way, just add water and time.

"With slot canyons, the water digs deep and fast, so the rain cuts a narrow path." They could feel the tires struggling to maintain traction as the walls closed in.

"It doesn't look like you get that much rain here," Chris said, staring out at the dry landscape.

"We don't, except for this time of year. It's monsoon season. We get heavy rains, dust storms, big lightning strikes. The weather moves quick and violent. The wind picks up and the sky goes dark. Next thing rain is falling like you've never seen. Then it's gone before you know what happened." Jake pointed to the canyon wall. "You get stuck someplace like this when it comes through, and you're not going to survive."

"So, if we're in monsoon season now, should we be driving down here?" Chris asked, looking at the high walls, imagining what they'd be like flooded with water.

Jake shrugged. "Probably not the smartest move."

He slowed a bit and rolled down his window, then leaned out and began driving at a crawl. "Something came through here." He pointed just ahead of them. "Look at that over by the rock wall. See that rut where the soil is pushed up? Couldn't be a truck or you'd see two sets, maybe a dirt bike, but it's so deep and wide, that'd have to be a heavy bike." Jake pushed the accelerator again, and the tires fishtailed until they gained traction.

87

Chris looked ahead as the sun dropped behind the rock wall. The cliffs were turning in, closing off the trail. Jake was still on the gas. A few yards from where the walls came to a dead end, he cut his wheel and turned the truck around, pointing it back the way they'd come.

He left the truck running and the headlights on. The sun was still out, but it was darker down below the walls. "Stay here," Jake said getting out. As soon his door was closed, Ben opened his.

"Ben, hey, Ben," Chris called trying to grab his arm, but he got out too quickly.

Amita undid her seat belt. "Where are you going?" Chris demanded.

"Out there," she said as if it should've been obvious.

"But Jake said to stay in the truck," Chris pointed out.

"Do you do everything you're told?" Amita asked, jumping out.

Chris undid his belt and slid to the door putting his feet on the ground, then he stayed, watching the others.

Jake was twenty feet away by the cliff wall where the rut he'd seen ended. He squatted down, looking at the ground intensely, touching the sandy soil, then scratching his head in confusion. Ben was halfway to him before Jake noticed the red headed kid. "Hey, I told you to stay in the truck," he called over his shoulder.

Ben didn't listen. He stepped next to Jake. "So, what do you see?"

Jake shook his head in frustration but didn't bother to argue. He let the sand run through his hands saying, "Whoever was pulling that diamond thing had it behind him most of the way, wiping out his tracks. . . Then just about here," Jake pointed to where the rut ended, "he picked it up." There was a set of footprints. Jake put his hand down into one. It was twice the size. "He's a big fella for sure." He stood up, following the trail with his eyes.

"That doesn't look like a foot or a shoe," Amita said. Jake and Ben hadn't noticed her joining them till that moment.

"I know," Jake looked down at the marks. "It doesn't look like anything I've seen before. Well, maybe that ain't true. If I were tracking Big Bird, the print would be pretty damn close."

He started following the trail, heading towards the canyon wall, to a dark shadowy spot in the pale rock face. He walked slowly, his eyes constantly on the ground. Just before he reached the wall, he stopped and bent down again.

"What is it?" Ben asked.

"It looks like he got behind it here, like he started to push it ahead of him down into the canyon," Jake pointed to the shadowy spot, the opening to the slot canyon, but his eyes immediately returned to the trail. "Man, that's weird."

"What?" Amita asked, who was now just behind Jake. Neither of them noticed Ben going ahead, slowly getting closer to the canyon's entrance. The opening was only a small break in the rocks.

"When he gets behind the thing, there looks to be a second set of prints, bigger than the first ones. They're right on top of each other. If those are his hands, this thing has got to be the size of a gorilla," Jake said.

"Hey, Ben, where are you going?" Chris called from the open door of the truck. He noticed Ben trying to sneak into the canyon entrance. He got out of the truck, heading towards Ben who jumped at the sound of his name, dashing ahead into the canyon.

Jake looked up in time to see Ben disappear. "Get back here!" he yelled, getting to his feet and hurrying after him.

Chris and Jake reached the entrance at the same time. "I swear I'm going to murder that kid," Jake said.

"Can't say I blame you."

As they stepped through the opening, Jake held his finger to his lips asking for silence, listening for Ben's footsteps. Chris would've gone quiet anyway as he stared in awe at the canyon. There was sunlight coming down from ninety feet above shining on the strangest landscape he'd even seen, full of bizarrely striated walls that seemed to curve and flow like a living thing. He touched the ridges on the wall closest to him, feeling how smooth they were after being worn by wind and water for millions of years.

"Stay with me," Jake said, placing his hand on Chris's shoulder. "It's easy to get lost in here." There were branches going off in different directions, some no more than three feet across. Jake pointed at the ground where Ben's footprints stood out clearly, following the broadest passage. They started off after him.

∞

Amita entered the canyon just behind the others, but neither Jake nor Chris noticed her. She stood at the entrance staring in amazement just as Chris had. The landscape felt alien. She looked up, wondering how far it was to the top. Her eyes sought the sun far above this, where she noticed something strange. Off one of the side branches, far from the canyon floor, maybe a third of the way to the top, something was reflecting the sunlight, shining and twinkling on a ledge.

In the distance, she could hear Jake and the boys. She knew they'd catch Ben soon. 'Jake knew the terrain and let's face it, it was Ben they were after,' Amita thought. 'Before long he'd see something shiny and get distracted.' She was aware of the irony as she debated over waiting for them, still looking up. 'But what if Jake doesn't want to check this thing out?'

Amita started down the side branch, her eyes never leaving whatever it was that was glinting in the sunlight. She was thinking of Joseph's story as she searched for handholds.

## Chapter Eighteen

Alex heard Katy yelling at the camera, "Just get her!" A moment later he felt hands helping him to his feet. He was able to walk a little.

Katy was on one side and his mother was on the other, "We'll get him into my office," she was saying. The bare walls of a gently curving hallway passed by. It was cool inside. The air conditioning felt good. His mother opened her door and placed Alex gently in the chair behind her desk. "You should be resting. Why would you come here?" she asked.

Alex was having a tough time focusing on her face. He shook his head a little hoping to clear it, but he instantly regretted the motion. "Where's Chris? We've got to get out of here. It's not safe," he managed to say, before pausing, waiting for the room to settle.

"I know, Alex, better than you do." His mom put her hand on his shoulder.

Alex's vision cleared further. He looked at her and Katy.

"But you have to understand that in a way I'm responsible for what Doctor Virtanen created here. It was my theory . . . from years ago. We didn't have the technology then. I didn't think we had the technology now, but somehow Doctor Virtanen was able to create it."

She glanced at Katy. "Your father is a good man, and a friend, but I think he may have overreached. . ." She looked at Alex, then took a deep breath, her eyes going around the room. There was little in it, a dry erase board with numbers that seemed to turn and twist strangely around themselves in a type of math that Alex had never seen before. There was a computer terminal and a family photo on the desk along with a stack of papers.

His mother's eyes stayed on the board for a moment, then she nodded before beginning again, telling Katy, "I never talk about it, but I'm sure my sons know that I've worked for the military —with things that are inherently dangerous. But what you have to understand is that there's so much oversight. In wartime, they may create something like a nuclear bomb, but the rest of the time they're just trying to stay ahead of the technology curve with processing speeds or stuff like stealth tech and drones. Something like this, a place like this, it's all privately financed. There's practically no oversight, nothing to stop them from pushing too far."

"That is enough Ellen." The deep European voice came from the hall. Alex and Katy both turned to see Doctor Virtanen standing there. He wasn't alone. Pacheco was with him, scowling with barely controlled rage. The medical doctor, Wallace, was there as well. Virtanen and Pacheco started into the room, but Wallace slipped around them to arrive first. "I need to examine the patient." He came to Alex's side, took out a penlight and placed his hand on Alex's head, lifting it back to shine the light in his eyes.

Alex didn't care for the way the doctor grabbed him. He didn't like being treated like a specimen. He grabbed the hand with the light and twisted it away.

"Don't touch me," he warned.

"Nice kid," Pacheco said from the door. "Maybe you should try that trick with me." He stepped into the room, approaching Alex.

"Leave him alone," his mother said, blocking the way.

93

Pacheco looked like he was ready to go through her. "I only want to talk to him," he said coldly, closing his fists in anticipation.

"That'll be enough," Virtanen said, "enough from everyone." He looked at Dr. Johnson. "You cannot tell them, Ellen. You know you can't." He turned to Pacheco. "And you —I think you've interrogated enough children this week."

Pacheco stared at Virtanen, "Fine, but he needs to go back to the med clinic. I'll escort him there if you don't mind."

"I'm not going anywhere with you," Alex said. "And there's no way I'm going back to that clinic. I saw the others, lying out like corpses. I'm not going to be another one of them for this guy to play with." He stared at the doctor with narrowed eyes.

Wallace backed towards the door holding up his hands and turning to Virtanen he said. "I'm taking good care of those people. All this boy really needs is rest. He can get that back in his trailer."

"I'll take him there," Katy offered.

Alex looked at his mother. "We can't stay here, Mom, you know that."

Virtanen came over and bent down in front of Alex, looking him in the eyes. "I need your mother here. I do not think I can do this without her. We're dealing with things that are much bigger, much more important, than anyone in this room," Virtanen glanced back at Alex's mom. She didn't say anything. She only nodded in agreement. Virtanen turned back to Alex. "She'll be perfectly safe here. I give you my word."

Alex stared at his mother. Finally, he nodded as well then struggled to his feet. Katy took his arm, and they started toward the hallway. Pacheco stepped aside but only after an uncomfortable moment.

Virtanen walked with them till they were out of the building, back in the hot desert air, then down past the dirt mound. "Keep an eye on him, Katy," he said, touching his daughter on her shoulder. He turned back to the observatory.

"It's not safe, Dad, and you know it," Katy called behind him.

Alex stayed quiet, staring angrily at Virtanen. Katy had to force him to turn away. "Come on," she said.

Alex moved slowly, feeling heavier as he leaned on Katy. In a low voice, he said to her, "I don't think we can trust any of them. I've never seen my mother so scared before."

# Chapter Nineteen

Amita listened to the others. Their voices echoed in the distance. 'It's hard sometimes, going unnoticed, and other times it's kind of nice,' she thought.

Standing on the canyon floor, the narrow walls made her feel tiny. She looked at the sand and saw the marks of something passing this way. It's up there. She could see the spot reflecting in the sunlight, knowing that it had to be the diamond object that had landed in Joseph Bizahalone's field.

'But how to get up there?' The walls were so smooth. Her hand ran over the surface till she felt an indent, a place where the stone was broken. There were more, going up the wall like a trail on the rock face.

"Wow," she said, imagining how the mark were made. Rock climbers used hammers to make handholds in stone walls, but these opening seemed larger. Something very forceful had torn into the sandstone.

Amita grabbed the first opening, pulled herself up, then reached for next one. It was sort of fun. She found the climb surprisingly easy. Small for her age, Amita was the type of kid whose parents always tried to get her to eat more and worried they could see too many of her ribs. Her size worked well for climbing though, as she lifted her tiny body higher and higher.

A significant mechanism of injury is more than three times a person's height, she remembered when she was halfway to the ledge, not sure if she'd read that in one of her forensics books or somewhere else. She glanced down. The thing they always say not to do. Surprisingly, she wasn't afraid. True, it did make her dizzy, but that only refocused her and made her climb faster, keeping her eyes on her hand holds.

The walls weren't straight. They moved in and out like waves climbing to the opening at the top. She was on a part of the wall that flowed out, forcing her to climb laterally beneath a rocky outcropping. It was the first time her hands started to sweat, the first time she felt apprehensive about what she was doing. The diamond thing was directly above her. Amita could almost see the edge of it hanging out over the rock ledge.

Forcing herself on, she followed the trail. The canyon had gotten much narrower here. Looking across at the other wall, Amita saw marks where the diamond had scratched into the rock, which made her think it had been used to spider walk up.

The handholds ended just before the ledge. The canyon was three feet across at its narrowest point, but Amita was still well below that.

On the other wall and above her, Amita saw a few shallow ridges below the ledge. She wondered if she'd be able to hold onto them. Her right arm stretched out and her fingers touched, but just barely. Straining, trying to reach a little further and twist, bringing her leg over, she let go with her left hand stretching toward the smooth surface of the opposite side. Her fingers touched, gripping with all her strength. For a moment it worked.

There was enough time to reach up for the ledge itself. Enough time to see the diamond lying on its side with its point aimed towards the last sliver of sunlight peeking over the lip of the canyon. Despite being covered with dirt and grime, the thing was beautiful in its strangeness.

The moment passed as Amita lunged, grasping and trying to pull herself up. Her hand slipped. Gravity took hold, and she was falling.

She felt her heartbeat once. A loud thump that pushed against her ribs while the rock moved away from her. She knew it was her that was actually in motion. There was the sickening sensation of freefall that seemed to slow time as she stared at the blue sky.

She lost track of the sun over the canyon rim as a dark thing slipped over the ledge. A massive form blocked the light, dropping down, falling towards her. Then something large and strong reached out and closed on her arm, stopping her in midair. She held her breath, glancing down at her dangling feet, then looked up and found herself staring into the strangest eyes she'd ever seen.

They were alien, colored like no creature on Earth with compassion sparkling behind them. Its face was vaguely bird-like with a long mouth similar to a beak and eyes set back on its head, small in comparison to its hulking size.

Amita glanced at the darkening ground certain the fall would've killed her. It was still mid-afternoon outside, but the sun had dipped so low that the canyon was in twilight. She looked back at the creature, knowing that if it wanted to, it could crush her bones. Her wrist hurt and she was grateful it didn't squeeze tighter and even more thankful that it'd saved her life.

"Thanks," she said.

The creature was hanging onto the ledge with one giant arm while holding Amita with the clawed toes of its leg, which was shorter than those massive tree trunk-like arms.

Gently it pulled her up, repositioning its legs around her waist. It was cautious not to squeeze too tight. Then it began to descend, answering her slowly, "Careful, careful, girl." He walked his arms down the wall and in a moment it had her on the ground.

It stayed up, clinging to the sides as it placed her gently on the sand and said again, "Careful, careful. It'll all happen once more." Its voice was steady, never changing pitch, measured out like the slow beats of a metronome.

It dropped to the ground in front her, and Amita felt a tremor through the sandy soil as the heavy thump echoed off the cavern walls. She stared at the creature, at its arms hanging down under it. They were almost as long as the creature was wide. Much of its body was armored and scaly like the hide of an armadillo, though the plates were smaller, allowing for free movement.

Amita took a moment to breathe, trying to keep her wobbly legs under her as it turned and started to climb back up again. "Wait! Where are you going?" she asked.

It stopped, turning its head as if it weren't sure what she'd said. "My busy glowing friend is here to stop it, but he's too late, always too late . . . he means no harm, but he wants to stop it all so bad, the thoughts and plans." It shook its head and tried to focus on Amita. "I'm sorry. I am confusion . . . the lights and the colors of the void . . . I wasn't ready for them . . . everything was touching," it answered in its achingly slow way.

It stared at Amita. It held up its hands almost pleadingly. "Understanding will take time." Then it pointed to its own head.

That's when Amita heard voices. The others were returning, going past the branch of the canyon Amita was in. She looked back and saw Jake, who was carrying Ben over his shoulder and not looking happy. Chris was ahead of him, going toward the cavern's opening.

"Hey, what are you doing down there, Amita?" Ben asked, looking back over Jake's shoulder. Then Ben saw the creature in front of her. "Look at that, it's right on her!" He managed to push off of Jake, falling on his face before getting up and charging towards Amita and the creature.

"Get back here!" Jake yelled, reaching for Ben as he followed him for a few steps. Then he saw the thing. Twilight was fading quickly in the canyon, but he could still see the large dark shadow looming over her.

Jake had seen mountain lions kill livestock and he'd chased coyotes away from his family's ranch before. His reaction to this creature, so close to the girl, was much the same. "Yaaagh!" he yelled, loud and primal, charging towards it, waving his arms and yelling again to scare the thing away.

Darting forward he grabbed Amita and started back towards the entrance. Shoving Ben's chest as he went, he demanded, "Come on, kid!"

Ben didn't run though. He picked up a rock and threw it, making a loud smack as it crashed into the creature's head.

"Wow, did you see that?" Ben said.

The creature startled and took a quick leap, landing on the wall.

"It's not dangerous. It was talking to me," Amita pleaded. Jake didn't wait or listen. Instead, he dragged Ben along by his shirt collar as he turned and dashed out of the canyon, heading back towards his truck.

"I can't believe I hit it! Man, I totally just saved you, Amita," Ben was saying.

"Just shut it, Ben," Chris ordered as he got out of Jake's way, following behind.

"It wasn't going to hurt me," Amita insisted.

Jake refused to listen as he carried her out of the canyon to the truck. He shoved her in, then grabbed Ben by the shirt collar and pushed him in next. Chris went around to the other door. He didn't need any encouragement.

"Just be quiet, all of you, just be quiet!" Jake yelled. "I'm getting you guys back to your parents." He started the truck and slammed his foot on the accelerator, leaving a trail of dust behind them.

## Chapter Twenty

Katy glanced at Alex. The couch was too small for him and his arm had dropped off the side. She thought about picking it up, but she didn't want risk waking him. He'd passed out not long after they got to the trailer. He and Katy had talked for a while after leaving the observatory, and he told her about the attack, giving her each detail. The thought that this creature could look like a person frightened her the most. After Katy told him about her own experience with it, they both agreed that it wasn't safe for anyone here anymore.

Eventually, their conversation turned. They were both heading into their senior year in high school, and the experience of being dragged off to the desert was something they shared. Alex complained about missing the last week of baseball. "Not that our team was any good. We had too many seniors who didn't care anymore."

Katy wasn't really into organized sports, but she was an avid surfer. "June's my favorite month. School gets out, and you've got a few weeks before the tourists descend. It's actually kind of gray in San Diego at that time of year, but that just gives you more waves to yourself." By the time she finished telling him about her favorite spots to surf and paint, he was out cold.

Alex was dreaming, 'probably about something unpleasant,' Katy thought as she watched his face tighten and release. 'He was a good-looking guy, but man, was he serious, almost like he'd been born without a sense of humor. Then again, she wasn't getting to know him under the best of circumstances,' she reminded herself. Katy always preferred being around people who could laugh a little, like her dad used to, back when her mom was still around.

Standing at the window, she watched the sun drop lower in the sky and the security lights flash on, well before the sun had set. Alex and the security guard were the first people attacked inside the fence. She couldn't see much of the facility, just the cafeteria building. She wondered if the creature was still out there, if it was watching them even now. It hadn't been interested in Alex specifically. From what he told her, it sounded like he'd been in the wrong place at the wrong time. He wasn't the one it was there for.

The guard sounded like he'd been sleep walking just like Troy. Alex hadn't seen the man's eyes, but Katy had a feeling, that if he had, they would've been the same as Troy's, glowing in that unnatural way.

Shaking her head as the memory came back, she wondered if anyone had reached out to Troy's parents. He was eighteen, but he still lived at home, so they were probably worried about him, wondering where he was.

She would've called herself, but it was impossible to get an outgoing line and cell phones were useless here. Katy felt awful as she thought about it. Troy had come for her, and now he was lying in a cold room, on the other side of that long building, not dead, but not really alive either.

She looked at Alex again. He probably didn't need someone to watch over him, but she stayed anyway. It was better than going back to her father's house.

There was a pile of books by the couch, mostly sci-fi stuff and fantasy. Katy sifted through them, looking at the cover art and wishing she'd brought a sketchbook with her. She picked one book up, glancing at the clock, then at the door. She settled down to read. Past dark she heard someone struggle with the lock.

"Hang on," she called, wishing there was a peephole as she cracked it open. Dr. Johnson stood on the other side.

"Thanks," she said, stepping past Katy. Dr. Johnson placed a white paper bag that sounded like a baby rattle on the table. She looked at her son. "I've got to wake him to give him his meds. The doctor wants him to take a course of antibiotics. He gave me something for the pain too."

Katy stayed by the door, looking towards the twilight sky at the soft dark colors of the sun fading across the desert horizon. She could see the gate in the distance, recognizing Jake's truck as it pulled beneath the bright security lights. "Looks like the others are back."

Dr. Johnson pulled the bottles from the bag. "I need to go get Chris," she said, glancing at Alex.

Katy watched the security guards surround the truck, opening the doors and escorting the passengers out. It was hard to tell who was who till she saw one of them try to run. That had to be Ben. "You just can't stay out of trouble, can you?" she said as she remembered her own time in the interrogation room with Pacheco. She hoped her dad wouldn't take as long to get her brother away from the security head.

Across the room, Dr. Johnson stood next to her son. She touched his face gently, but his eyes stayed closed. "He looks so peaceful. I wish I could let him rest some more," she said.

Katy closed the door. "I can hang out for a bit longer while you go check on your other son. I'd get Ben, but I'd probably wind up being detained myself. If Alex wakes up, I'll give him the meds," Katy went to the table, looking at the three vials standing there. She picked one up and read the name.

"These are sleeping pills, really powerful ones." She looked at Doctor Johnson. "My mom used to be on them. The doctor doesn't want him to take these with the pain pills, does he?"

"No, those are for me. I've been having trouble since I got here. And even when I manage to fall asleep, I get up feeling more tired."

"This place has that effect on you," Katy said. "Just go easy. Like I said, they're really strong. They'd knock my mom out for a whole day sometimes. Of course, they had her on so many other things."

Doctor Johnson nodded and looked at Katy with her eyes full of compassion. Katy wasn't sure how much the scientist knew about her mom. Her dad didn't like to talk about his wife's mental breakdown to his colleagues, or what happened after. Katy was young then, but she still remembered how it went. The way people stopped calling. The way living with someone so damaged isolated her and her family. When her mom was actually gone, it was almost easier. She hated thinking that, but she'd been so young, too young to be a caregiver.

Dr. Johnson smiled at Katy and touched her on the shoulder. "Thanks for watching Alex." As she left, Katy held the door. She closed it and her hand lingered on the knob for a moment. Knowing it wouldn't do much, she twisted the simple lock, then sat down and started reading again. But she had trouble focusing on the words.

# Chapter Twenty-One

Amita sat at the dinner table with her parents. It was a later meal than usual, and her father wasn't happy about that. Dr. Patel liked to do things on a schedule. He liked precision. Her mother, the other Dr. Patel, had prepared Malai Kofta and Jeera rice, but the Malai Kofta wasn't fresh. Her mother had made a large batch of the vegetable balls a few days before, keeping the sauce separate till it was ready to be served. Her mom, like her father, was a talented engineer, but despite that, they maintained certain traditional roles in their home. It was always Amita's mom who made dinner, and they always ate it together.

Her father hadn't said anything about the meal being late, but he didn't have to, making his annoyance clear by his silence.

"Aren't you going to say something?" Amita asked.

"Do you need me to say it again, to tell you how disappointed I am that you'd sneak off with those two boys, leaving like some sort of hooligan?" Her father's voice was controlled and eloquent while simmering with anger.

His disapproval hurt Amita. She loved her father very much. In many ways, he wasn't only her dad but also her closest friend. At CERN in Switzerland, and here in the Arizona desert, her father, even with his busy work schedule, spent as much time with his daughter as possible. They worked on science projects, discussed books and articles and played strategy games that she'd devised. He'd even taught her to fly fish in a stream in northern Italy.

Amita remembered that day, wishing she were back there now as she said, "I went with them because you two won't tell me anything. All this secrecy is ridiculous when people are getting hurt." She touched everything in front of her, moving her fork and her bowl around, fumbling with her napkin, then added softly, ". . . And I was— I was curious." She looked up at him hopefully. "You've always said that was a good thing."

There was a glint of pride in his eye, but it went away quickly, turning cold as he dove into his plate, not saying a word. It was the deepest wound she could imagine. It was the same look he'd given her when he entered the security office.

Pacheco and his men had pulled Chris, Ben, and Amita from the truck and ushered them into the room. Amita was certain they would've been separated if there had been more space. Jake was the only one placed by himself. He was held in Pacheco's personal office.

"Have a seat. I'll get to you in a moment," Amita had heard the security head tell Jake as he slammed the door before coming into their room. He closed their door and twisted the lock on the knob.

There was a desk secured to the floor and three heavy chairs, no windows and a florescent light flickering overhead. Pacheco clutched his hands behind his back and asked, "You saw something out there, didn't you? I want you to describe it."

"Which part?" Ben asked.

Pacheco paced the small space, stopped and starred at Ben coldly, as if the answer should've been obvious.

Ben shrugged as he started to respond, speaking way too fast. "Well, there was a white buffalo, which I've never seen a regular buffalo before, so that was really cool. Then there was that giant diamond thing, though we didn't actually see that. We just heard about it from Jake's uncle. Oh, but Amita may have seen it. You said you did. Right, Amita? Of course, the biggest deal was probably that thing in the slot canyon. By the way, the slot canyon was pretty cool in itself. I'd never seen one of those before either but—"

"The thing in the canyon, that's what I want to know about?" Pacheco demanded.

Ben looked at the others, giving them only a half second to answer. "Amita saw it the best. I only saw it a little. It was the size of a bear, though I've never seen a bear up close before, so I'm not sure if that's exactly true, but you know take it for what it's worth—"

"Alright, just stop, be quiet for a minute." He pointed to Ben before turning to Amita. "I want to know what you saw," he demanded as he leaned down on the table.

Since leaving the canyon she hadn't said much, trying to commit to memory and analyze what the creature had told her. She tried to collect her thoughts.

"I don't think it's here to hurt us. I mean I don't think it's the thing that's hurting people here. It's something different," Amita said.

Suddenly Chris's mom came banging on the door. She stormed into the security office with Amita's father not far behind. Pacheco tried to send them away, but then Dr. Virtanen arrived as well. "I don't think you'll be interrogating any more children tonight. If you want to talk to them, then you can do it in the morning. And you'll be doing it with their parents!" Dr. Virtanen's face was red.

Amita, Chris, and Ben left with their parents, but as Amita walked out, she couldn't help looking back at

Pacheco's office door, knowing that Jake was still inside. It wasn't fair that his night would probably be the longest of all of theirs. Amita was still thinking about him an hour later as she ate dinner with her parents, while also wondering about what the alien had said, still trying to remember his exact words.

She wanted to talk to her father, to tell him everything, but he didn't look like he was in the mood for listening. He was still focused on his meal, slipping his knife through the Malai Kofta, although it was soft enough to be broken with a fork. Finally, after a long stretch of painful silence, without looking up, he said, "I'm going to take the morning off from work. I'll be driving you to Flagstaff."

"Why?" Amita asked.

Her father's eyes came up and met hers. "You're right that people are being hurt," he said. "But this isn't some Scooby-doo mystery for you and your friends to solve."

He turned his attention back to his plate, cutting again. "You're going to be flying out in the morning, first into Phoenix, then back to London to stay with your grandmother."

"But..." Amita began to say. She wasn't sure how to even begin protesting.

Her mother touched her hand, saying softly, "There's no point in arguing. Our work here is too important. I'm sorry, but this is how it has to be."

"But it spoke to me," Amita pleaded. "I was falling, and the thing out there grabbed me, and saved me. It's something new. Something no one has even seen before. It's wonderful, and it was communicating." She looked from her mother to father.

"What did it say?" Amita's mother asked.

"It doesn't matter what it said," her father interrupted. "In the morning Pacheco will go out to see if anything's there. I may even allow you to answer some of his questions before he goes, but for now, it's best if you just put this stuff out of your head. You never should've been here, not after the explosion. It's not safe."

"But Dad—"

"Enough! This conversation is over."

Amita looked at him but didn't say anything. She turned away, asking to be excused, hoping she could leave before her eyes had a chance to well up.

## Chapter Twenty-Two

Chris hadn't been stuck with the security head long, but he got the sense that something bad had happened. His mom hadn't said much until they walked outside. When they were alone, she told him about his brother's attack.

"You can't be running off like this. It's not safe here." His mom's voice shook with concern. Amita's parents were there as well, but they stood apart, waiting for the main gate to open.

"Mom, what is it?" Chris asked as the chain links rattled in front of them. The lights on either side of the gate were blinding. Amita and her parents hurried off while Ben and Dr. Virtanen hadn't come out yet.

Chris's mom waited till they were alone then said, "Your brother was attacked." Her arm was on his broad shoulder, moving him forward.

"What?" Chris asked, not sure if he'd heard her right. Then she filled him in on how they found Alex unconscious by the fence. "He was cut. It was almost surgical. Any deeper and he would've been eviscerated. There's been other attacks too. A guard was with Alex. He was injected by some sort of poison, a paralytic. He hasn't woken up yet." She was matter of-fact in the way she said it. That was how his mother dealt with terrible things, by looking at them objectively.

"Is Alex going to be, okay?" Chris was thinking about when he'd left in the morning with Ben. Maybe if he had stayed there, Alex would've gone back to bed. Or maybe if he'd gone running with his brother, like Alex was always trying to get him to do, the creature would've finished with the guard and left already. Alex certainly wouldn't have been able to run as fast if Chris were with him.

"He'll be fine. He needs to rest and heal, that's all." She hugged Chris tight once they were through the gate and out of sight of the guards as she tried to hide the tears in her eyes. "What were you thinking? I was so scared."

Chris didn't have an answer so he did the only thing he could. "I'm sorry, Mom."

She hugged him again as he mumbled into her shoulder, "We saw something out there." He wanted to say more, but he was struggling. He hadn't seen the thing in the canyon himself, not very well anyway, so it was hard to describe. Instead, he asked, "What is going on out here?"

His mom looked at him, then shook her head. "I only know a little. But there's one thing I'm sure of. It's not safe, and you guys need to leave."

They made their way across the grounds. Just before reaching the trailer, she added, "I'm going to work on getting you and Alex out of here in the morning. I have to try and find someone you can stay with."

Chris grabbed her hand. "Seriously, you're not leaving?"

"I can't," she said, opening the door and walking in. Chris followed her, ready to argue some more, but then he discovered they had company. Katy was sitting by Alex under the light of a single, softly glowing lamp, reading a book. It was one of Chris's.

"Hey, welcome back," she said, looking up.

Smiling awkwardly Chris nodded. He had trouble coming up with words, so he pointed at her hand,

"Book," he said, followed by, "Um, hi."

Katy turned it over and looked at it. There was a girl on the cover surrounded by Dragons. "Yeah, I hope you don't mind. I wanted something to pass the time, I'm not usually into fantasy, but this looked cool."

Chris hadn't officially met Katy yet, but he'd been thinking about her since the other night in the security office. She'd been covered in dirt and tears, torn up from the night before and Chris thought she'd been pretty then, but now, all cleaned up, he was having trouble focusing. "It's not fantasy," Chris blurted out more harshly than he meant.

"What?" Katy asked looking back at the cover. "It's got dragons."

He softened his tone. "Um, yeah but the dragons are an alien species. The whole series is about a lost human colony that lives with them in the distant future."

"Okay, well I don't read a lot of Sci-fi either," she said.

Chris smiled then he glanced at his brother, the way too handsome Alex. Of course, he had a pretty girl sitting next to him. 'This guy has got all the luck,' Chris thought. Then he saw the bandages peeking out from beneath his brother's shirt and felt his jealousy slip away. He pointed. "Is he alright?"

"He's stayed asleep the whole time," Katy said, getting up.

"Thanks for keeping an eye on him," Dr Johnson said. There seemed to be something unspoken between his mom and Katy.

"No problem. Did my dad get Ben yet?" Katy asked.

"Yeah, he was there. He was probably the only reason we were able to get the kids away from Pacheco."

Chris tried not to groan at the word, 'kids.' While Katy glanced at Alex, "There goes my dad, making everybody's life easier again." She looked at her page and closed the book. "I suppose I should get home for my brother. I'm sure my dad doesn't want to watch him."

Chris's mom looked at her sadly, but didn't say anything, only nodding. As Katy headed for the door, she turned to Chris, holding the book up. "Do you mind if I borrow this?"

Her strawberry blond hair flipped over her shoulder, causing Chris to pause before answering, "Definitely, sure. . . I mean I don't mind at all," he stammered.

As tired as Chris's mom was, she couldn't help laughing a little. She turned away, trying not to embarrass Chris more.

"Thanks," Katy said, ignoring his stammer and smiling as she left.

As soon as the door closed, Chris looked at his mom who was still smiling.

"What?" she asked while shrugging. She had a glass of water and a number of pills in her hands. She went to Alex's side and rubbed his arm till he woke up enough to take the medicine. Alex had to be helped into his bedroom. They both took a side and walked him slowly.

"Where've you been?" Alex mumbled to his brother.

"I told you Ben wanted to go hiking. Turns out that's not really my thing, too much walking," Chris said while holding his brother's arm.

Still foggy, Alex stared at him for a moment. Chris expected some sarcastic comment about his weight, but instead Alex shook his head. "You need to stay close. It's not safe out there." He undressed and climbed under his covers. Then Chris shut off the lights and left his brother, going to bed himself an hour later after trying without success to get more information from his mom.

He told her about what happened in the canyon. Told her about what Jake's uncle had seen, but she hadn't shared any information of her own. She just sat there listening quietly. At one point she shook her head. Chris thought she disagreed about what he'd told her, but then she whispered, "How could he be so stupid?" She slapped her hand down on the table, then got up and went to the kitchen to take a pill.

"In the morning I'm going to do everything I can to get you guys as far from this place as possible, then I'm going to make some phone calls. People need to know about his experiment. It needs to be shut down. If that's even possible."

Chris tried to ask her what she meant, but she wouldn't say anymore. She went to her door saying, "Goodnight, baby. I love you," before closing it.

He went to bed himself, falling asleep to the sound of his brother's slow, steady breathing. When he woke a few hours later, he listened, hearing a different sound.

Someone was moving around in the trailer. He heard kitchen drawers opening and closing. Chris looked over at Alex's bed and saw bunched-up sheets, left in a pile. He looked at the clock. It was three in the morning. For a moment he was tempted to roll back over, but then he thought of his brother, cut up and wounded. He forced himself to sit up and go to the door.

There was a single light on below the microwave in the kitchen. Chris could see his brother there, rifling through the drawer. There was the sound of metal being shuffled around. "What are you doing?" Chris asked.

Alex didn't look up at first. He was focused on the drawer. Then he finally found what he was searching for. His hand came up holding a long, sharp kitchen knife. Alex touched the edge, then gave it a practice jab, saying, "I heard a noise."

He stabbed the knife again and practiced pulling it back in a defensive position. "If it's that thing— if it's coming back for me, I'm going to make sure I'm ready." His face tightened as he winced in pain holding his hand to his stomach.

"You should be resting," Chris said.

"I know, but we're not safe here, none of us." He walked around the counter coming towards Chris and passed him the knife, handle first. "Hang onto this, okay?"

Agreeing, Chris nodded, but he had a hard time imagining using it as a weapon, especially against something the size of what he'd seen in the canyon. Of course, Amita was convinced that whatever they saw there wasn't the creature attacking people. Alex had seen something different, he wouldn't admit it, but he was scared. The frantic tone in his voice was something Chris had only heard when their dad was in a mood.

Alex opened a closet door, again looking for something. "I'd have to get too close with the knife to do any damage, but maybe you can at least protect yourself with it." He came out holding a baseball bat.

"This is more like it."

He gave a little practice swing, wincing again. Chris went to steady him. Alex held the bat with one hand and his belly with the other. "I won't be hitting any home runs, but it's better than nothing." Alex motioned to the closet. "Grab one."

Chris squatted down feeling around for his brother's bat bag. While in there he heard Alex walk toward the window and pull the blinds aside. "What the hell is that thing? Come here and look at this," Alex demanded.

Chris didn't have to ask what he meant. He felt it again. That angry buzzing, the insect sound he'd heard the night before, was coming up through the floor. He knew his brother was seeing that same light, the strange glowing below the windowsill.

Pulling a bat from the bag, Chris was surprised by how much better he felt with its weight in his hand. He stepped back, looking towards his brother, who was still at the window and getting ready to open it.

"Don't!" Chris yelled.

Alex glanced at him, but before he could say anything there was a sudden crash. Everything rocked and moved as if they were in an earthquake. The walls and the floor shifted and shook. Plates fell from the dish rack and papers came sliding off the kitchen table while the chairs tumbled about.

Something hit their trailer right outside their room.

Chris put his hands out to keep his balance, thinking the whole trailer was going to tip over. It felt like a truck had crashed into them.

The brothers looked out the window at the same time. The light was brighter and moving, flying up over the next trailer. For a moment Chris thought he saw the fluttering wings of a dragonfly, but they were massive, at least two feet long, shining too brightly for him to see details. Then in a moment it was gone, leaving him half blind with the afterglow burning his eyes.

He tried to rub the blindness away as he turned towards his brother, who was doing the same.

Suddenly the whole trailer bounced up, lifting off its supports. Something large slammed up from below. The carpet, plywood, and steel sheathing were wrenched up into a small mound in the center of the living room.

Alex looked down for only a moment, then turned back to the window where something else was moving. He held his breath for a moment, then pointed and called, "Chris, look. It's there!"

Just outside the trailer, low and on all fours was a monster. It was black, but they could see the long blades on its arms folded back as it scurried along the ground. They watched it leap up onto the trailer next to theirs, climbing like a spider. Then it went over the top, disappearing as it followed the light.

Alex turned back to his brother, his eyes searching. Without saying a word, he asked if Chris had seen it too.

Chris nodded, feeling his whole-body tense.

"That was it," Alex whispered. "It was here. Right under us." He pointed to where the carpet was pulled up into a mound, then started toward the door.

"Where are you going?" Chris asked, following behind him.

Alex paused at the entrance. but he didn't answer. Instead, he forced himself to step outside. The metal steps rang loudly with every footfall. "Look at this," he called.

Chris stared at the open door, at the night sky beyond it. He took a deep breath and squeezed the bat a little tighter before following his brother outside.

Alex leaned down to examine the trailer, pointing to one of the blocks that the supports sat on. There were scrape marks from where it'd been pushed.

The two brothers stepped out into the street, watching as the light dove and flew around the trailers in the distance, chased by the black thing. Chris's eyes stayed on the sky till the light disappeared, noticing how dark the night was. There was no moon, and the stars seemed to have vanished.

A strong wind blew, carrying dust from the road into their faces. In the distance, a crack of lightning filled the blackness revealing dark clouds forming like a wall. "There's a storm coming," Alex said.

"A monsoon," Chris answered. He hurried back up the stairs, remembering what Jake had told him about the storms, how quick and violent they could be, but he couldn't worry about that now because something had dawned on him. Through all that, his mother hadn't woken. With all that noise and the trailer nearly being knocked over, she should've come out by now. "We need to check on Mom," he said.

# Chapter Twenty-Three

Amita's eyes were open, staring at the ceiling. She was tired, exhausted really, but couldn't sleep, unable to calm her mind. Reading didn't help. After several different books, her thoughts still wouldn't settle. They wandered back to the canyon, back to that creature.

'How could they not?'

Filled with an incredible urge to go back there, she looked at her clothes neatly piled on a chair and thought about putting them on. She plotted how to do it, going out the hole in the fence, hot wiring that old pick-up, then following the trail that Jake had driven.

Then she remembered the look of disappointment on her father's face and her stomach twisted. Sitting up and going to the edge of her bed, she thought of her grandmother. Her flat in London was tight, hot and smelly. Amita never enjoyed staying there. Her grandmother watched TV at a volume that bypassed her ear drums and drove the sound of talk-shows directly into her skull.

The quiet in the desert was something she was going to miss. She looked around her room and thought it might be a little too quiet.

Amita got to her feet and went to the door. She didn't really have to go the bathroom, having gone a half-hour before, but it was something to do as the night moved slowly past. Maybe she'd even stop by the fridge and see if her dad had snuck some ice cream in there.

She didn't turn on the lights as she went into the dark hallway. The bathroom was directly across from her door, next to an empty bedroom. The stairs were to her left, and her parent's room was to the right at the end of the hall. A picture window above the stairs let in the glow from the streetlights shining in the circle outside their house. Its square panes of glass made a twisted shadow like an elongated net lying over the carpeted floor.

In the bathroom, Amita closed the door in the dark, waiting before reaching for the light. That's when she heard a sound from down the hall. There was a loud thump in the direction of her parent's room, then another. She stuck her head back out, looking at their closed door.

Another thump, then she heard the knob turning.

It twisted back and forth, not quite far enough to open. Whoever was on the other side was struggling with it.

'Two engineers and one of them can't figure out a door,' Amita thought. She was certain it was her dad, probably half asleep, going for ice cream too. She'd picked the habit up from somewhere.

Amita came back into the hall and debated over going into her room, but something held her there in the hall waiting, wanting to see her.

Her parent's door opened slowly revealing her father's silhouette. He stood unmoving.

"Hey, Dad," Amita said in a low voice. "I was just going to the bathroom." He didn't answer.

Amita blinked a few times, struggling to see better, steadily realizing that something was very wrong. Dread filled her. When she looked into his eyes, she saw that a soft glow shone beneath his half-closed eyelids, unblinking, staring past her. She froze in place, staring at her father.

Just over his shoulder a shadow stepped forward. Amita saw her mother's long dark hair half covering her face. Her mother's eyes were lost beneath the dark strands, glowing with the same unearthly light.

Her parents moved forward, shuffling slowly at first, their faces completely passive.

"Mom, Dad it's me," Amita said as they came closer. She was standing still, not sure if she were unwilling to get out of their way or if she was unable to, frozen with fear. They came on in single file. "Please answer me," she begged, finally moving back a little, one small step at a time, till she reached the stairs.

Her dad came close enough for her to smell his skin. Amita stared into his vacant eyes, then felt his hands land on her, taking a firm hold. Amita closed her eyes, trying not to cry as with a jarring motion he lifted and dropped her on the floor.

She collapsed to the ground, not because of the force he'd used, but because Amita couldn't get her trembling legs to hold her. Every breath felt stretched out as she listened to them move past her door. She sat frozen and isolated.

From the floor she watched her parents start down the stairs. They struggled with each step as if they were a complex problem to solve. Her father nearly fell, then reached out for the handrail. Her mother did the same thing a half second later. Their hands moved almost in unison.

Amita stared at their backs, hoping this was all a dream. Then something called her attention. At the window, a light was moving a little, glowing bizarrely just below the sill. 'It's back,' she thought, watching it, "and if it's back. . ." she said out loud. Amita thought of what happened to everyone else who'd become one of these glowing-eyed zombies. They were the ones being attacked.

She sat up, her eyes still on the window, on the fluttering thing out there. It seemed like it was trying to stay close to the house, hiding in the eaves. She looked at the stairs, seeing her parents begin to turn. 'My parents,' she thought, 'they aren't who I need to be afraid of.'

Her resolve stiffened as she got to her feet. She sucked down her fear, knowing she had to stop them.

They reached the landing halfway down. Amita followed. "Guys, you've got to wake up!" she yelled.

They stepped onto the ground floor with Amita right behind them. Her father reached out for the front door; this knob was less of a struggle.

He swung it open as Amita grabbed her mother's hand, pulling back. "You can't go out there. You can't! You've got to wake up!" she screamed, tugging with all her might. Her mom tried to shake her loose, but Amita held on with both hands.

Her father turned and slowly came back. He grabbed his daughter again, this time more roughly. With a cruel jerk he twisted and pulled her hands away, then lifted her and threw her into the living room.

Amita was small for her age. She flew through the air, smashing hard onto the floor. Her breath was forced from her lungs as her head whipped back and crashed.

By the time she looked up, her parents were both already outside, moving off into the night. Amita struggled to her feet, feeling dizzy. She coughed a little. Everything hurt. Her elbow, her shoulder, and her head.

A strong wind had started, and the desert dust was blowing into the house through the open door, stinging her face. She went out onto the front step, looking up at the buzzing just above her head. The glow crept over the ledge, but whatever was making the noise was hidden by the roof line.

"Stop!" she called after her parents, but they'd already gone into the circle. They were still moving, stomping on in a straight line towards the observatory.

"Please stop," she cried again, watching their shadows lengthen in the streetlight, getting further from their home. Plans and ideas ran through her head, but they vanished from her mind once she saw they weren't alone. It was too late. The hunter had arrived.

It came from between two houses like an apparition made of blackness, large and moving quickly, crossing the circle on all fours. It leapt and pounced on her parents, knocking them both to the ground. Amita could see the creature as clear as day under the lights. Its skin looked artificial, like the side of a stealth fighter, going between dark gray and black matte. The thing rippled with muscles and striated tubing that pumped and throbbed below its skin.

Even though the long blades were out, it didn't bother to use them, dropping its broad head over her parents. A thick, ropy, tongue came darting out. The attack was so quick that even if her parents had the will to struggle, they wouldn't have had time.

The creature stood over their bodies and glanced back at her. Deep black eyes focused on her for a moment, then it charged.

Watching it come closer and closer, Amita wanted to turn and run, but again she felt frozen. She thought she'd be joining her parents, that she'd be the next victim. But before the monster could crashed into her, it jumped and landed on the roof above her. As clay shingles rained down around her, she tried to get out of the way, falling back onto the step and covering her head.

From her back she watched the light come flying out of its hiding place. Wings fluttered as the black thing chased it. The light was struggling up the roof line, just clearing the peak as the creature reached out to grab it.

The high winds made havoc for the flying thing. It started in one direction. Then with a gust it was forced back towards the houses. The dark creature jumped from one roof to the next, following it.

The glowing thing dropped low, coming towards the ground just above Amita's parents. It gained some speed in a down draft, diving hard and flying over the fallen bodies, soaring back towards the complex, heading in the direction of the trailers.  Amita watched it go before running to her parents. When she took her father's hand and touched her mother's face, she started to cry, feeling how incredibly cold they were.

## Chapter Twenty-Four

The lightning struck and Katy counted, "One one thousand, two one-thousand, three one-thousand . . ." she got to fourteen, then did some quick math in her head. Sound traveled five seconds a mile, which meant the storm was almost three miles away to the north of here, towards Page. The last time she counted she'd gotten to twenty. That'd only been a few minutes before. The storm was moving fast.

The wind rattled her windows. Above the sound she heard someone knocking on the front door. They had a doorbell, but apparently whoever this was didn't care to use it. Katy looked over at her alarm clock to see what time it was, finding only a dark spot where the numbers should've been.

Her father's footsteps echoed down the hall. "Calm down, calm down" he called. His pants were half on as he tucked his shirt in and tightened his belt.

Katy got up and opened her bedroom door a crack after hearing him on the stairs. Their house was set up the same as Amita's, with the front door at the bottom of the steps.

She saw her father reach for the light switch, flipping it up and down and cursing a little when nothing happened. The power was out, but light came in through cracks around the front door. Dr. Virtanen opened it to find a truck parked in the circle with brightly shining headlights glaring at him. Pacheco was there waiting impatiently with his hands on his hips.

"What is it?" Dr. Virtanen asked and leaned around Pacheco, seeing security men pushing a gurney to the back of the truck while Wallace, the medical doctor, supervised. There was a body lying on it, carefully covered by a sheet. "What's happened?"

"There's been another attack, the Patels this time. Both of them," Pacheco said, pointing back over his shoulder. "Happened maybe twenty minutes ago."

Virtanen rubbed his hand over his forehead, started out the door, then stopped to ask, "Where's their daughter Amita?"

"We haven't been able to find her," Pacheco said. "We searched the house, and we're going over the surrounding area, but there's no sign of her. She's probably scared, hiding somewhere."

"You need to find her. Your men are not to stop looking."

"Understood," Pacheco answered. "But there's another matter to address. As you can see, the power is out."

Virtanen stepped back inside and pulled his shoes out of the hallway closet. "I know," he said shortly. He sat down on the side of the couch to put them on. "The Patels, are they the same as the others? In some sort of coma?" he asked.

"Yes, both stung in the neck. They're breathing, but that's about it. They'll be taken to the med lab," Pacheco answered.

Virtanen seemed to be talking to himself as he stared at the floor for a moment. "At least this stage of their work was nearly done. We planned to do some testing. See if it would absorb the stray exotic matter. But it's Dr. Johnson's work that matters now," he said, standing up.

Another lightning strike lit up the sky. For a moment, the entire complex was bright as day. Virtanen reached for the light switch again, flipping it back and forth in frustration. "These storms are a terror," he said. Heading outside, he glanced up the stairs as Katy ducked to the side, hoping to stay hidden. "I'm going to go to the generator building first to make sure everything is working there."

Pacheco stepped back out of his way. "According to protocol you're to immediately prepare the secondary device for deployment if we lose power," he pointed out.

"I know. I wrote the damn protocol." Virtanen shook his head, then considered his options. With a heavy sigh, he stared at Pacheco. "Fine, I'll go to the observatory first and make sure the device is prepped." He pulled on his jacket and grabbed a set of keys. "It'd be a terrible thing if we had to use it, though . . . Ellen is so close. If anyone can give us control over the singularity, it's her. There's not much point in tearing a hole in space if you can't control it." He went out, closing the door behind him.

Staying where she was, Katy listened to her father's pick-up start. When his headlights moved across the windows, she turned to go back to her room. That's when she discovered she wasn't alone. Ben had knelt behind her, staying quiet. Their eyes met.

"Did you hear that?" Katy asked.

Ben nodded.

"Where do you think she'd go?" Katy asked.

"We should check Chris's. She's not going to go to security and she's not going to want to be alone. If she didn't come here, then he's the only friendly face I can think of," he said.

"Then let's go find her," Katy answered.

## Chapter Twenty-Five

Stranded by the storm, the creature was hiding, finding it impossible to fly in the gusting wind. On another world, in another place, his species were called Lightning Bugs, a name they were given by a different people. Their true name could only be expressed in color and light.

'This weather is unexpected,' he thought, but how can anything be unexpected when the whole universe is repetition, full of moments that feedback, again and again, falling on each and tumbling forward. By instinct he knew the way, time and space folded on themselves, reaching out in an infinite number of directions. With such clear vision, he should've been able to predict his current circumstance, but there was always chaos, simple chaos. From when the winds decide to change, to when a little girl decided to empty her bladder, moment to moment the universe proved it was unknowable.

That girl, he hadn't meant to hurt her, but trying to dream-walk two people at the same time wasn't an easy task. The second event was coming, he could feel it. Time was getting short, and somehow these people kept getting in the way.

Those two back at the house would've been useful, but they were the girl's earlier generation. Her parents they're called. The little girl cared about them, enough to risk her own safety. The concept of family was strange to the Lightning Bug. At one time, when there'd been more of them, his entire species had been his family. Each one a brother and sister, touching each other's thoughts. But they were gone now. Almost all of them murdered. Some he hoped had escaped the purge and were in hiding, but he couldn't be sure.

Hiding wasn't an option for him. The hunter was here. It was a ghost given form, and it was close. The Lightning Bug wouldn't stop trying though. If he kept the second event from happening, if he could close the void from this side, then perhaps his people would survive, perhaps he wouldn't be so lonely.

∞

The rain hadn't started yet, but Ben and Katy could feel it coming in the air as the wind whipped around them. In the distance beyond the lights on the fence, they could see the darkening sky swallowing the valley. The security lights still had power, but only every third one was glowing. It was a different kind of light too, a softer, orange glow.

The dome of the observatory was dark, looming over them like a giant with its massive foot ready to fall. Squinting because of the dust, Katy stared, noticing the way the wind moved around it, the way the gusts seemed to break on it.

'It's probably really dumb to be here,' she thought as they crossed the abandoned grounds. Not a single soul was around. The facility felt evacuated, but she knew it was only because it was the middle of the night. Everyone was huddled in their trailers, most not even aware of the power outage.

She glanced past the observatory toward the generator building. The lights were glowing brightly there, and she could hear the subtle sound of giant machines carried on the wind. That noise would've been deafening up close. The five diesel engines supplied enough power to run a small city, but almost all of it was going towards the dome.

Ben and Katy walked toward the community center. All the windows were dark except for one on the far end in the medical center. The shades were closed, of course. They were always closed, but Katy could picture the inside, her friend Troy still laid out on a cold gurney with the Patels next to him. Doctor Wallace examining them, probably happy to have new specimens in his collection. He might be running out of room.

Katy thought of Troy's parents again, wondering how long her friend had been missing. She did the math. It'd been days. She promised herself that the first thing she'd do when she got away from here would be call them. Of course, she had no idea how that would happen. Plans were running through her head when she stopped in her tracks, staring at the cafeteria windows. Something was moving in there.

The lights were out, but she saw something.

Ben glanced back at his sister. "What is it?" he asked.

Maybe it was just the change in air pressure, but Katy felt the hairs on the back of her neck stand up. A chill colder than the desert air ran down her spine. Something was wrong. She was certain they were being watched.

"We really shouldn't be out here," she told her brother as she started walking again. This time faster, staying as far from the community center as possible.

Her eyes never left the windows.

'Had something moved inside? Or was that her imagination?'

They came to the trailers, going past one row after another. Even though she'd been here earlier, it was hard to tell which one was the boy's. They were all so similar.

"Five down, right?" Ben asked, heading toward it. "It's this one, I'm pretty sure." He scratched his head. turning to his sister. "Does that look off to you?"

Katy had been following her brother, but her attention stayed on the cafeteria, so she didn't know what he meant.

Ben motioned with his hands, rotating them in the air, "It's crooked," he said.

She didn't need Ben's help to see that the trailer had been knocked off-center, no longer lining up neatly with the others. "It wasn't like that earlier," Katy said.

"What could've done that?"

"Something big and not good," she answered as a fat raindrop fell, smacking her forehead. A few more drops hit the ground, quickly absorbed by the thirsty soil.

"I guess we'll find out," Ben said, picking up a stone. He cocked his arm back ready to throw it at the boy's window, but his sister grabbed his attention.

"What was that?" Katy's eyes darted back to the community center. She pointed to where she'd seen a spark of light. With his head turned, Ben saw it too. Unfortunately, the rock was already out of his hand flying toward the window.

"Ouch!" someone yelled.

Katy and Ben both turned back to the trailer. Chris was leaning out, rubbing his forehead. "What the hell, dude?" he shouted.

"Sorry, man. I wasn't expecting you to be there, I swear."

Chris rubbed the side of his face. "We heard you guys talking. We're on high alert around here." He held up his baseball bat.

"Is Amita in there? Her parents were attacked," Katy asked, still looking over her shoulder, watching the community center.

"Yeah, she's inside. She got here a few minutes ago, but that's not the only thing." Chris sounded distracted, glancing back in the trailer. "There's something wrong with my mom . . . something not good. She's talking in her sleep and, well . . . you'll have to see the rest. Just get in here." There was a slight tremor in his voice as he disappeared. Katy and Ben looked at each other before going to the door, not sure what to expect.

## Chapter Twenty-Six

The wind was becoming more violent, shaking the trailers. Katy and Ben struggled to keep the door from banging as they came in. Chris grabbed it for them and closed it, then went around the counter to his mother's room. He stood beside it, looking in. There was an odd silence in the trailer while the wind howled outside. Katy looked around at the others, but no one spoke.

Alex had something bright and glowing in his hand, a cell phone. He held it low, pointing it at the ceiling where the beam bounced off and made a cone of light. He placed it on the table. "Can't make a call, but I've kept it charged anyway," he explained before joining his brother by the door, putting his hand on Chris's shoulder. The two looked at each other but stayed quiet.

Amita was sitting at the table, her eyes were glassy, and her face swollen from crying. Upset, she looked up at Katy and wiped her cheek. There was a seriousness to her that Katy found frightening in someone so young. "We came here looking for you. Security is pouring over this whole place trying to find you." Katy said, not sure why she was speaking so softly, but feeling as if she'd just intruded on someone's wake.

"I suppose it would've made it easier on your dad and Pacheco if I'd stayed next my parent's bodies," Amita shot back.

Not sure how to respond, Katy kept quiet. Ben answered for her, "Yeah, well, obviously it would've been easier." He lifted an eyebrow and shrugged.

Amita shook her head. "I didn't feel like answering their questions." She stared at Katy. "What? Did your dad send you to come get me?"

Katy wanted to tell Amita what she'd overheard, but she was distracted. A sound was coming from Dr. Johnson's bedroom. Nearly lost beneath the blustering wind, there was a voice, a low mumbling that was impossible to understand.

Chris said his mom was talking in her sleep, but the voice on the other side of the door sounded nothing like Dr. Johnson's.

It was a murmur full of discord, as if the voice making it had never spoken before. The noises went from a low range, steadily becoming high-pitched, then turning into something more like buzzing.

When Ben wandered over to her bedroom, Katy noticed a light coming from inside, glowing around the edges. She was about to follow him, to find out what was happening but Amita stopped her, saying, "She's like my parents." Katy stared and Amita continued, "Her eyes, that's what my mom and dad's looked like just before the attack."

Katy thought of the night she'd tried running away, the way Troy had looked, the way he'd acted.

Slowly, she started toward Chris and Alex. Even in the dark, she could see the concern on their faces. She stepped past them, going just inside the door. Dr Johnson sat on the edge of the bed. Her back was rigid as she stared forward with unblinking eyes that no longer had irises or pupils. A bizarre glow had replaced them.

Katy's hand flew to her mouth. 'Had it only been three nights since she'd seen someone with eyes just like this? Could she really have forgotten how strange it was?' Of course, she'd only seen Troy for a moment. She hadn't gotten to stare at him like this. Dr. Johnson wasn't moving, except for her mouth. The sounds were still coming from her, those terribly strange wave lengths of inhuman clamor echoed out. Katy remembered earlier when this woman had looked at her in such a kindly way.

Ben interrupted her thoughts. He was standing right behind her. "Well, if she's a zombie, then she isn't your regular kind. She should be attacking us by now, trying to eat our brains or something."

"Do everyone a favor and be quiet for a little while, Ben," Chris said, grabbing him by the shoulder and pulling him back. He'd seen Alex's jaw clench and his fist tighten. His brother was on edge and he didn't need Ben pushing him over.

Katy took a deep breath. "Has she tried to move?"

"No, she's just been sitting there," Alex said.

Katy watched Dr. Johnson's mouth. It was out of sync with the sounds coming from it. Her face stayed passive though, almost serene. It was beyond disturbing.

"My dad said he needed her." Katy turned to the others. "Whatever this project is, whatever he made, he needs her to get control over it."

Ben nodded in agreement and turned to Amita. "Pacheco came to our house just after your parents were attacked. Katy and me listened in on his conversation from the top of the stairs."

"What exactly did he say?" Amita asked.

Katy backed out of the room, keeping her eyes on Dr. Johnson till she passed the threshold. "He said your parents' work was almost done. They'd created some sort of equipment that needed testing. He said it had to do with absorbing exotic matter." Amita's eyes widened, causing Katy to stop, waiting for her to say something.

Amita motioned with her hand, urging Katy to keep going. "He was worried that something would happen to your mom." Katy turned towards the boys. "He said they couldn't control what they made here without her."

"He called it a singularity," Ben interrupted.

"He called it a tear in space too," Katy added. "It sounds dangerous."

Amita was quiet for a moment, then she nodded.

"I'd certainly agree; if it's true, it's proper dangerous. He's balls-up for sure. I have to wonder about the exotic matter though. As far as I knew, physicists were just now working on detecting the stuff, proving the particles even existed. If my parents built a machine that could absorb them, then I'd say they're well beyond simple detection. That's rather important. They should've been publishing, winning awards for it."

"So why haven't they?" Alex asked suspiciously. "Because they took the experiment further," Amita answered. She turned to Katy and Ben. "Your father did something with those particles." Amita went quiet for a moment, her face locked in concentration as she tried to remember something.

Ben broke the silence, coming over to the table and blurting out, "What did he do?"

Amita ignored him, looking toward Alex. "That would be the part where your mother comes in. She's a theoretical physicist who's worked for your government for years, correct? Well then she's probably had access to data that very few scientists are granted."

"My mom's a patriot. She'd never give out secret information," Alex said.

"But they went to school together," Chris reminded his brother. "Her theories, the ones Dr. Virtanen was so interested in, were from before she went to work for the government."

Amita stared at Chris, waiting for him to make one more leap. When he didn't, she filled in the rest. "Alright then, so what if those theories are why she went to work for the government in the first place." "What do you mean?" Alex asked.

Amita pushed back from the table and stood up. She came over to the others and spoke with the voice of a teacher. "Have you noticed how small computer processors are now? How small machines that think have become?" She didn't wait for anyone to answer.

"There's a point where simple circuits and physics, like in nuclear physics, intersect, a very tiny point.

"When it comes to military applications, the government is always trying to make their weapons smarter and often that has to do with making them smaller, their processors you see. The brain of every machine on earth is on the threshold of becoming subatomic in size.

"Physicists, like your mother, live in that world. They study it, make theories about it; try to understand something so very small. But in a way, it's like another universe when you get down to that scale. And there are other things there, things that people have only theorized about.

"Maybe when your parents worked together, maybe they came up with some way of detecting those things."

"What are you talking about?" Alex asked.

"I'm talking about wormholes or the Einstein Rosen Bridge. They're openings in space-time that lead from one place to another. People in fiction have been traveling through them for years."

Chris looked at his pile of books in the corner, certain that he could find at least a few wormholes in there.

Amita leaned against the table, crossing her arms. The others had come closer as they listened intently. "Those stories may be made up, but mathematically, according to the theory of relativity, they are possible," Amita said. "The problem is that they're so small and last such a short amount of time that they've proven to be undetectable." She looked up at the others as she finished, saying, "I think your father may have used exotic matter to try and create a stable wormhole. And I think that's what is under that dome out there."

"And that's bad?" Ben asked.

Amita shrugged. "I don't know. I mean he's using something called 'exotic matter,' to disrupt a force of the universe that we know almost nothing about. Think about that name, 'exotic matter.' In other words, it doesn't behave like normal matter. Anything could happen."

"So basically, their father is risking all of our lives," Alex said, glaring at Katy and Ben.

"Basically, he's risking the whole bloody world." Amita stared at Katy.

"Hey, your parents knew just as well what they were. . ." Katy started to say, but she stopped midsentence.

Her back was to Dr. Johnson's bedroom door. She heard someone moving there. Slow, shambling footsteps dragged across the floor. Katy glanced over her shoulder.

Dr. Johnson passed through the doorway, coming toward Katy. The scientist's eyes were glowing, and her mouth still made those bizarre sounds. Slowly a pattern began to develop through the murmuring. Dr. Johnson moved forward with unsteady steps as words began to form. In an inhuman voice, with long drawnout syllables she said, "Help . . . me . . . Please, help . me . please, help me please, help me please, help me please." She repeated it again and again like some bizarre chant.

## Chapter Twenty-Seven

Ben was the first react. Or, more accurately, overreact. "The Zombie is going to get us!" he yelled as he dove behind the table landing at Amita's feet.

Katy moved back as well, only startled. Unlike her brother, she fought back her fear, watching the women she'd spoken to a few hours before, come toward her. Halfway across the room, Dr. Johnson stopped and went silent. She stood in one spot, swaying a little.

Chris, Alex, and Amita stared in disbelief while Dr. Johnson's glowing eyes followed Ben. She watched him hide behind the table before rotating slowly and falling on Katy. Then Dr. Johnson made a sound very much like the word, "Fear?" The voice was high pitched and painful to listen to.

Katy met the glowing eyes that shined beneath a mop of disheveled hair that cast strange shadows, distorting Dr. Johnson's face. Her mouth moved again, and this time it was clearer when she said, "You, fear?"

Now Katy was certain that it was asking her a question. She also realized that she'd thought of Dr. Johnson as an 'It,' knowing there was something else behind those eyes. 'It,' was controlling her. Just as 'It' had controlled Troy a few nights before and Amita's parents earlier.

Katy glanced back at Amita, who hadn't moved. Amita glared at Dr. Johnson, aware as well that there was another presence in command. Outside the wind was still screaming and they could feel the trailer moving with it. Everything felt unstable. "Yes, I'm afraid. You've hurt people," Katy said.

Dr. Johnson turned her head, looked at Amita before coming back to Katy, "Help me please," it said.

Then it added, "Help me stop this, please."

"What happened to my parents?" Amita asked as she pushed past the boys to stand beneath the glowing eyes, looking sickly in the pale light. "What did that other thing do to them? How do I help them?" she demanded.

Dr. Johnson's head shook back and forth, her eyes glancing down only for a moment at Amita, "Food storage," it said. "The hunter is coming— I can't fly. Help, please." The words drifted slowly off as her eyes began to dim and the glow went away.

Dr. Johnson's knees folded and she started to fall. Alex and Chris grabbed her arms to keep her from hitting the floor, but Alex grunted, grabbing his stomach while his face twisted. He had to let go, so Chris reached around, taking both her shoulders and slowly lowered his mother down. Kneeling by her side, Chris brushed her blond hair back from her face. "Mom, can you hear me?" he asked. There was no answer.

He leaned close to make sure she was still breathing. Her chest was rising and falling, and he felt her breath on his cheek. "Mom!" he called again, shaking her a little. Her head turned, and she moaned.

Her eyes fluttered, but she refused to wake up.

Amita took the phone from the table and came closer, shining the light on Dr. Johnson's face. "She's not like the others. She wasn't stung." Amita kneeled next to Chris and touched his mother's arm. "She's breathing faster than my parents were and her skin hasn't turned pale or icy."

"She may just be sleeping," Katy offered. "She took a pill earlier. It was a pretty powerful one."

"This powerful?" Chris asked. He lifted her arm and let it drop.

"Maybe being possessed wore her out," Ben said. "I mean it's gotta be exhausting, being a zombie." He looked a little embarrassed for running away.

"She's not a zombie," Chris said, having trouble finding Ben in the dark.

"Well, maybe not in the traditional sense—" Ben started, but he was cut off.

"Just stop! It's enough already," Katy shot at her brother as she leaned down next to Chris, looking at his mom. "Zombie isn't the right word anyway. It's more like she was possessed."

"What? Like by a demon or a ghost? Are we going to need a priest? Does anyone speak Latin?"

Everyone stared at him till he stopped talking.

"I'd say whatever possessed them was something that came through the wormhole, an alien. I think it's that glowing thing," Amita answered.

Chris nodded. "They were under the trailer just before you guys got here. The big one nearly knocked us off the foundation." Chris pointed to the pushed-up spot in the center of the floor. Amita shined the light on the twisted mound of carpet.

Alex added. "That was the one that cut me. The one that can disguise itself." He looked around the room. Even in the dim light, he could see Katy was the only one who understood what he was talking about. "Before that thing attacked, it looked like a person. I couldn't tell who it was, though."

"I noticed it was wearing pants when it attacked my parents," Amita said nodding.

"It didn't go after you?" Chris asked.

"No, it was chasing that light," Amita answered.

"And I was an inconvenience," Alex pointed out. "I think he came after me because I saw him change. It probably didn't want that information getting out."

"So now, it's the glowing one asking for our help?" Amita's voice was bitter.

"It said, 'food storage.'" Katy went to the front window, looked out. "I thought I saw something move in the cafeteria. Maybe we should start there."

"But what's it trying to do?" Amita demanded. "Why does it possess people? Why did it take control of my parents, or your friend, or the other victims it led to this monster?"

"It's just a guess, but I think it wants to shut down the wormhole. I think that's the whole reason it's here," Chris said, glancing around at the others, but unable to see their faces in the dark.

They were quiet for a moment till Ben spoke up.

"If this wormhole is as dangerous as Amita says, then we should totally help shut it down. Besides, this hunter thing is obviously kind of a tool. I mean, it tried cutting your brother in half, and it put the whammy on her folks. That's total tool behavior."

Amita looked like she wanted to say something, but Ben hadn't finished. "Oh, but you know what else I was thinking," he said. "There aren't just two of these guys running around. There's the third one." He turned to Amita. "Remember your friend out in the canyon?"

"What canyon?" Alex asked.

Chris looked up at his brother. "That hike was more interesting than I made it sound," Chris said before briefly filling him in on what they'd seen.

Katy had heard the story from Ben, but Chris was able to recite it with much less flourish and Amita filled in a few more details. She told them how it had saved her, then recited his words verbatim, "My busy glowing friend is here to stop it, but he's too late, always too late. He means no harm, but he wants to stop it all so bad, the thoughts and plans." She looked around at the others, waiting for someone to say something.

Alex made his way to a chair. He was holding his stomach as he sat down. "The one in the canyon may have come through the wormhole too, but right now he's out there, out of the way. We need to decide what we're going to do about the two that are here now." "We help the glowing one, of course," said Katy.

"Why?" Amita asked.

Katy turned toward her, confused. "It's being hunted. The other one is hurting people. It's hidden among us, and it's going to keep on hurting people till it's stopped."

Amita crossed her arms. "Yeah, but it wouldn't be if the glowing one weren't taking possession of them, basically making them into mindless—"

"Zombies?" Ben shouted holding his hand in the air like answering a trivia question.

"For lack of a better word," Amita said.

Alex turned his attention to her. "Yeah, but it's also trying to shut down the wormhole. Aside from the danger of having a tear in space, it's also, more than likely, how these creatures got here. If the glowing one knows how to shut it down, then we should at least try to talk to it. Help it if we can, before more aliens decide to show up. Worst case, we gather some intel."

"Or we all get turned into Zombies," Ben said.

145

"I don't think that'll happen," Amita answered. "I don't think this creature can control you if you're awake. There've been five attacks, each one at night. The first was a technician who liked to go backpacking in the desert, often sleeping under the stars. The second was Katy's friend who'd driven through the night from San Diego. He may have been sleeping in the truck waiting for her."

"The security guard I saw could easily have been catnapping out by the containers," Alex added.

"And then there were my parents. They were home in bed. . ." Amita looked off as she said it, letting her thoughts go elsewhere.

Alex had put his baseball bat down by the wall. He went over and picked it up again. "Well, if this is what we're doing."

Chris's bat was near the counter. He glanced at it, then down at his mother. "Do you think you could help me get her into bed before we go?" he asked Katy.

There was a slight tremor in his voice.

"Maybe you should stay here, Chris," Alex said, touching his brother on his shoulder.

Chris moved around to his mother's head, getting himself in position to lift her. "Besides you, I'm the biggest guy here. And you're still hurt. You're not exactly in the best condition for a fight."

Alex glanced at the others, then he nodded. He and Katy went to Dr. Johnson's legs. Luckily, their mom wasn't a very large woman. Strong for his age Chris was able to lift her upper body without much trouble. He laid her in bed gently, even taking the time to bring up the covers up.

Chris came back into the living room. Ben, who was holding a frying pan, and Amita were by the door. She hadn't opted for a weapon. "Where do you two think you're going," Alex asked.

"With you," Ben said, giving a practice swing with the pan.

"Yeah, I don't think so," Alex said.

"But—" Ben started to say.

Katy cut him off. "I don't want to hear it. Alex is right. You two need to stay here where it's safe."

"So, why's he get to go?" Ben said pointing to Chris, "We're the same age."

"Yeah, but he's tougher," Alex said. "And we want to do this as quiet as possible."

Despite everything going on, Chris felt himself swell with pride. He'd never heard his brother saying anything like that about him.

"Ben, you're staying," Katy repeated. "Hopefully, we'll be back soon." Ben looked at Amita, hoping to find an ally, but Amita stayed quiet, handing the phone to Katy. The battery was significantly drained, so Katy shut it down while Amita, stepping away from the door.

"Hang on a second," Ben said and placed something from his pocket in Katy's hand. "What's this for?" she asked, holding up a key.

"It goes to pretty much everything but the observatory," Ben answered.

Katy looked at her brother, expecting more of an explanation.

"It's a master key. It'll get you into the community center or any of the secondary buildings." "Where'd you get that?" Chris asked.

I stole it off my dad's keychain a few nights back so I could bust into the cafeteria after hours."

Katy shook her head. "You really need help." Then she hugged him before leaving with Alex and Chris.

## Chapter Twenty-Eight

While Ben stood in the entrance, the gusting wind tried to pull the door from his hand. He watched the others go toward the community center. 'This sucks,' he thought. He hated being left behind, but he wasn't going to fight with his sister about it. He didn't have many people in his corner. In fact, he could only think of one, and that was Katy. If she wanted him to stay, then that's what he was going to do. He watched Chris, Alex and her cross the road, and all he could do was hope that she'd be alright.

Heavy raindrops hit the trailer roof, echoing loudly, and were absorbed into the thirsty ground. When the boys and Katy disappeared around a corner, Ben closed the door. It was dark inside since Alex had taken his phone with him. He could hear Amita going through the kitchen drawers, rifling through them, looking for something. Maybe a flashlight or a candle.

"Whatcha doin?" Ben asked. She didn't answer, but when her hand came up, she held something that looked more like a steak knife. It was certainly pointier than a flashlight.

A lightning strike lit up the room as she came around the counter. Ben closed his eyes, then rubbing them he felt her move past him. The front door opened. The rain sounded even louder than before.

"Where do you think you're going?" he asked.

Amita closed the door, passed by him again, and went to the closet. "Hey," he said. reaching out blindly, touching her shoulder and hoping she wouldn't stab him.

She shrugged his hand off. "I'm going to try and get help," she said while searching in the dark again. Her hand closed on a raincoat that was too large for her, one of Dr. Johnson's, but she pulled it on anyway.

"The security guy is going to lock you up in one of his interrogation rooms. You're better off staying here," Ben said.

Amita passed by again. "I'm not going to security. I'm going to find an expert on aliens." "Who's that?" Ben asked.

Amita swung the door open, saying over her shoulder, "An alien of course. There's one sitting out in that canyon."

Ben could see her outline in the entrance. He reached out and grabbed her arm, this time with a stronger grip. "You're going back there?"

Amita stared at Ben's hand for a moment. "It saved me, and it was trying to tell me something," she said. With a quick twist of her wrist, she broke his grip and stepped down the front stairs.

"How do you plan on getting there?" Ben asked, following her into the rain, instantly regretting that he hadn't grabbed a jacket himself.

Amita kept walking. "I've got a plan," she said holding up the knife.

"Well, you can't go by yourself," Ben called. He was holding his hand above his eyes, trying to see her through the rain.

"You better come with me then," she called, still not slowing down.

Ben stood frozen for a moment, watching her get further away. Amita moved like a miniature speed walker, pumping her arms as rain sprayed off her coat. Shaking his head, he went back up the trailer's three steps.

Before he closed the door, he listened for a moment to see if he could hear Doctor Johnson's breathing, but the sound of the rain was too heavy. He went back to the front door, reached around and locked the knob, then took off jogging after Amita, calling, "Hey, wait up!" He hoped Katy wouldn't be too mad at him.

∞

The wind whipped the rain across Alex's face. Following Chris and Katy, he was moving as fast as he could while bent over in pain, feeling the stitches pull at his wound. He'd end up back in the medical center under Doctor Wallace's care if he kept this up. But he wasn't willing to let Katy and his brother go without him.

He'd seen what this 'hunter' could do.

Alex knew he'd gotten lucky last time. Surprise had been on his side. The monster hadn't expected a kid to be fast or to have any sort of training. Even then, he'd come out like this, nearly cut in half.

Watching his brother ahead of him, Alex's hand tightened on his bat. Chris had some fight in him, Alex knew that. They'd squabbled often enough over the years. Smacked each other around, as brothers do, and Chris could hit hard, but he also tended to give up.

Alex had seen his brother crack, put up his hands, and even start crying. Of course, that was when they were younger. But even as teens it could be embarrassing to watch him flop around during his wrestling matches. Chris never tried hard enough to win. Of course, Chris only wrestled because their dad expected him to compete in something. Sports weren't really his thing. Alex looked at him moving next to Katy. Chris was almost two years younger than her, but a head taller and twice as broad.

He probably had thirty or forty pounds on Alex, and despite the hard time he gave him, Alex knew it wasn't all fat. Chris was a strong kid, but that wouldn't matter if they ran into that monster.

They ducked under the awning when they reached the community center. All three were soaked from the rain. The water pummeled the earth, forming a curtain that was hard to see through. The awning was five feet deep, but it did little to keep them dry as the wind pushed the water in, soaking them further.

Alex watched Chris pull at his shirt. He could tell his brother wasn't happy with the way it was sticking to him, clinging to each fold and roll. He noticed the way Chris was trying to avoid staring at Katy as she went to the door. She was soaked through as well. Seeing his embarrassment, Alex felt bad for Chris. His little brother was so awkward around girls, and even here, facing alien monsters, he looked like he was ready to jump out of his skin. Alex patted him on the shoulder. "You alright?'

Chris looked surprised. "Yeah, I'm good," he said as Katy unlocked the community center door. He and Alex followed her in. The air conditioning immediately made them cold.

The door closed behind Alex, and while they could still hear the storm outside, it was much quieter. The thumping of the raindrops formed a constant white noise that was duller than the squeaking sound their sneakers made on the tile floor. The sound echoed off the empty walls, causing all three to stop in place. They looked at each and listened. Then their eyes went over the hallway.

Glowing red light came from emergency exit signs, shining off the polished floor. There was light coming through the cafeteria windows that ran the length of the hall looking in on the dining room. Thin curtains covered the windows, but a faint glow still seeped out.

Alex pulled at the door. It rattled but wouldn't open.

"Let me," Katy said in a whisper.

She felt around in the dark, then pulled the phone out of her pocket. She handed it to Alex, who turned it on, keeping it low and pointed at the lock. Ben's key worked and the door swung in with the hinges squeaking for oil.

Inside, the cafeteria was brighter, but not by much. There was a light back behind the counter. Emergency power was being fed to the glass fronted coolers where the drinks and sandwiches were kept.

"It said 'food storage.'" Chris pointed toward the counter. None of them moved at first. They were staring across the room past the tables and chairs.

Katy took a deep breath, saying, "Okay." As she took the first step forward, trying not to let her feet squeak, the brothers fell in behind her, each holding their baseball bat.

Katy looked back at them. "If I get turned into a zombie, you guys better not be planning on hitting me with those," she whispered.

Chris immediately lowered his. "No, of course not," he said.

Not moving his bat a single inch, Alex kept his attention on the kitchen. He wasn't worried about zombies. He was worried about the thing that hunted them.

They came around the counter, entering the kitchen where the light from the coolers reflected off the stainless-steel appliances. In the center of the room were serving stations that during the day held buffet trays.

153

They took up most of the floor space along with tall metal shelves that were stacked high with mixing bowls, pots and pans.

Large stove tops with vented hoods lined the back wall. Past that was a small hallway with alcoves cut into it. Carts that held trays of dishes, cups, and silverware were crowded back there.

They could hear the hum of a large freezer at the end. Alex came around the corner of the buffet stations, moving slowly toward the hall. He held the cell phone light up to see better while going past the first dish cart. With Katy and Chris in single file behind him, his eyes were on the freezer, a large subzero unit for storing meat with a digital readout on it.

The wind and rain got louder as they moved further down the hall. Above that, was a banging sound, moving with each gust. It was the sound of a door that hadn't been closed tight enough.

Alex whispered over his shoulder, "Someone came this way."

Passing the third and final tray of dishes, he noticed another room to his left and turned, pointing the phone toward it, only to see boxes of pasta, tubs of sauce, and loafs of bread.

A light pulsed once and faded inside the room. Then it started to move, coming forward, toward him, floating on wings a meter wide in the beam of Alex's light.

Alex jumped back, dropping the phone. The light went out, but the room remained bright as a creature hovered in the center. Strange colors twisted and turned around it. Alex's bat came up, but Chris jumped forward grabbing his arm before he could swing.

Chris glared at his brother till Alex pulled the bat away, "I'm fine," Alex said, never taking his eyes off the thing in the room.

Katy put herself between the brothers and the alien, moving in with slow steps. "Hello," she said hesitantly, "Were you the one who contacted us?" She kept her voice soft, but it was impossible to hide her nervousness.

The creature was similar to an insect with a head, thorax and abdomen. Its flesh was like a jellyfish's, cloudy and clear in spots, with bioluminescent light running through its whole body. The spindly appendages coming off its center appeared too small to be useful. Wings twice the length of its body moved so fast they were nearly invisible. Only their glow and their buzzing gave evidence they were there.

Slowly, in response to Katy's question, it nodded its head, which rested on an elongated neck. Broad, glowing eyes were staring at her from a smooth, oval face. Its mouth was a tiny line that spoke, saying,

"Help me. Please?"

Katy was in awe, watching the lights of the creature's body. It was beautiful and filled with colors.

"Help you how?"

Before it could answer, Alex demanded, "What have you done to my mother?"

The creature turned its attention to him. It was impossible to determine emotion from a face that was so alien, but Katy thought she sensed sadness. "No harm," the creature answered.

Alex thought about its words before asking, "'No harm,' to you or 'no harm' to my mom?"

It shook its head. "No harm to mother. She dreams. I walk in dreams to stop the void. To close it before it swallows all." It turned to Katy, motioning with those tiny arms towards its mouth. "Your world swallowed and gone. Bad for all worlds, destruction will follow. It must stop!"

It looked past Alex towards Chris, "Mother will wake again, but world will be gone. Event happens soon," it said.

"What event?" Chris asked, not caring for the way that sounded.

"I think it means Earth. It's worried the whole planet will get sucked into the wormhole Amita was talking about," Katy said, glancing back at him.

"Well yeah, then we definitely should help him . . . it, I mean whatever this thing is," Chris said motioning towards the creature.

"Lightning Bug. I am Brash," the creature said.

"Brash, that's your name?" Katy asked. The creature nodded again.

"If we're going to shut the wormhole down, then we've got to speak to my dad. He needs to hear what you have to say," Katy explained. Brash nodded again.

"You think he'll listen?" Alex asked.

Katy was about to answer, but then there was a noise behind them, the sound of a door opening and closing.

Suddenly the light from the creature began to change. The glowing turned from mellow pinks and greens to deep shades of purple and red. "It's here. The hunter," Brash said in a low voice.

Alex felt his stomach sink. Then he took a breath and stepped back into the hall. "You need to get Brash out of here. Get him to your dad," he told Katy.

"What are you going to do?" she asked.

Alex was making decisions, weighing options. When he came to a conclusion, he looked at his brother. He knew he couldn't do this alone. Alex needed back up. As Chris nodded to him and lifted his bat, Alex tried not to notice Chris's hands shaking.

"We're going to try and buy you some time," Chris said, following his brother.

"Go out the back way and be careful," Alex called over his shoulder to Katy.

She watched the boys go, then opened her mouth to call after them, but shook her head instead. The longer she waited, trying to convince Alex that he was being stupid, the more chance there was of Brash being caught. She started toward the back door, turning and waving for Brash to follow.

## Chapter Twenty-Nine

The rain washed down the hill in a sheet, carving channels in the sandy soil. Ignoring how muddy and wet they were, Amita only cared about reaching the pick-up truck. Ben had slipped and fallen on the hill, not far from where his sister had been a few nights before. Somehow, Amita made it to the bottom without incident and slid to the passenger's door while Ben went to the driver's side.

He was about to get a foot inside when Amita asked, "What are you doing?" She pushed him out, then reached up and turned on the dome light. It wasn't very bright.

"Getting out of the rain," Ben answered. He was going to sit on her if she didn't move.

"Not yet," she said, holding her palm up towards his face. Ben stared at her, but she ignored him as she climbed across the bench seat. Ducking down and going headfirst into the driver's foot well, she jammed her steak knife into the plastic cover on the bottom of the steering column and tore it off. Rain poured in through the open door. Amita looked up at Ben.

"Close that," she ordered.

Ben made a face before shutting the door. He looked in through the window, trying to see what she was doing, but the glass was fogging up. As he stood there, tucking his hands under his arms, he looked miserable.

There were cables bundled in the steering column, and Amita's eyes immediately went to the red ones, the battery wires. The steak knife wasn't the best tool for stripping them, but she made it work, pulling them loose and cutting the covering back a half inch from the ends.

Next, she twisted them together, being careful not to let them touch anything metal.

As the wires connected, power went to the dashboard and the radio came on. Loud hip-hop music boomed from the speakers, drowning out the rain. A base tube smuggled beneath the seat was set at a volume that rattled Amita's teeth. She jumped back, banging her head on the steering column. It throbbed as she worked her way onto the seat and reached over to kill the CD player, ready to tear the thing out of the dash. She sat rubbing the back of her skull till a tapping on the window broke the silence.

Ben opened the door and stuck his head in. "Was that Ludicrous? I love old school hip-hop. He's the guy who was in all those Fast and Furious movies, well not all of them, but—"

Amita grabbed the door and nearly took Ben's face off closing it. Then she ducked back into the wheel well, grabbing the starter wire and carefully bringing it to the battery wires. Sparks flew as she touched them together. With the third strike, the engine came to life. Amita pushed on the gas a few times, revving the engine, then stopped and listened to it idle.

She sat up about to get behind the wheel, but Ben opened the door again and plopped down heavily in the driver's seat. "Nice work," he said. Water dripped off him, soaking the interior.

"What do you think you're doing?" Amita asked.

"What's it look like? I'm driving."

"What makes you think you're going to drive?" Amita reached over to open Ben's door and push him out.

Ben held the door closed, "I'm the only one who can see over the steering wheel."

"Barely," Amita crossed her arms, staring at him.

Ben motioned to the wheel. "Look, have you ever driven before? And I don't mean a remote car."

"I've driven . . . a golf cart anyway, and a four-wheeler." She was looking down.

"Yeah well, I have more experience than that . . . I may have borrowed my aunt's car a few times. That means I trump you," Ben said, reaching for the shifter and looking forward through the foggy windshield. "Man, I can't see anything." He turned on the wipers, but the glass wouldn't clear.

Amita reached for the defroster. The heat came on slowly, and the cloudiness went away. "See, now that's teamwork," Ben said, stepping on the accelerator.

"Just try not to drive us off a cliff," Amita answered.

∞

Katy followed the Lightning Bug to the back door, which was swinging in the breeze. It was stuck open, the lock no longer capable of latching. She looked at the mechanism. The door had a push bar, but it'd been disassembled, hanging down in the opening with springs and screws strewn about on the floor.

Glancing at Brash, she wondered if the creature had been the one who broke it. She wasn't sure how he could have with such small arms. As she pushed the door open, she felt the rain that was carried in on the wind. Brash had been hovering a few feet above the ground, but as the gusts came through, he struggled to stay aloft. His wings buzzed louder as he tried to fly.

"Help me," he begged.

Katy reached toward him. Seeing his soft translucent flesh, she was worried that she might hurt him if she grabbed too hard. He worked to gain height, coming near Katy's head. Then his wings stopped moving, folded around him and became opaque. He stalled in the air and dropped into her arms in a cocoon made from his wings. His face peeked out like a swaddled infant's.

"Are you alright?" Katy asked. There was nothing to him. He felt nearly weightless although he was still over a foot long.

Brash nodded. "Safe with you."

Katy looked out the door, wondering where she should go first. She needed to talk to her father.

"A device," Brash said, his head turning toward the observatory. "Atomic explosive. If void stays small, might be energy enough to break connection. . . unsure. . . But hope. Our best hope. Father needed for it."

"My father is our best chance . . . If you can convince him," Katy said, surprised by her doubt. "I dream walk?" Brash asked.

Katy was confused for a moment, then she understood, "What? You want to possess him? No way. We're just going to talk to him. Okay?" Brash nodded in agreement.

Katy was about to go out the door, but then she stopped looking down at him, "What I don't understand is why you haven't taken him already. If my father is the best chance . . ."

"He has to dream. He has to sleep. He hasn't. Not very much."

Katy nodded, feeling bad for her dad.

Through the open door, she looked up at the observatory, trying to see the path through the rain. Just about to step out, she glanced back the way Chris and Alex had gone, towards the kitchen. 'Did she hear them talking to someone?' She wondered if maybe things weren't that bad. 'Maybe the Lightning Bug was wrong, and it wasn't the hunter out there.' Then she heard a crash. She heard Alex yelling.

"We must go!" Brash said.

Katy felt her heart jump as she ran out into the rain. Holding Brash tight she dashed up the muddy trail toward the observatory. But then she saw headlights going up the road. There was a white pickup truck heading towards the generator building. "That's my dad!" she said as she whipped around and started heading toward the open garage doors at the generator building.

She glanced over her shoulder, back at the windows of the cafeteria and saw the blinds moving violently. Something was happening in there, something bad. She called for her father, hoping he'd hear above the rain and the sound of the generators, "Dad! Dad, help!"

# Chapter Thirty

The monsoon was moving fast across the desert. In Page, it had knocked out powerlines at midnight, and by one in the morning it passed over the observatory, catching everyone in the downpour. An hour after that it was in the mountains around Flagstaff, leaving the desert full of deep, sandy puddles and disturbed soil. Those temporary bodies of water reflected the headlights of the 4x4 truck Amita had hotwired. Ben drove, struggling to see as they bumped along backcountry trails through a dark, starless night.

"Do you even know where you're going?" Amita asked.

"I may not be as smart as you, but I've got an amazing sense of direction. I never get lost," Ben answered.

"Really?" Amita asked, watching him squint as he looked forward.

"Yes, really—I mean, almost never," Ben answered, while rolling down his window. "I'm nearly, completely, positive this is the way Jake came when he brought us back. There should be a turn around here somewhere."

Ben let the truck slow down, limping along over the water-filled ruts. Amita didn't want to admit it, but Ben wasn't a bad driver. His confidence could be annoying sometimes, but right then it was reassuring.

"You really think that thing in the canyon is going to help us?" Ben asked as he touched the gas a little.

He was cruising along slowly, studying the terrain.

It took Amita a moment to answer. "I don't know, but I hope so."

"You're worried about your folks, aren't you?" Ben turned toward her.

"They're all I've got, and I just can't imagine. . ." Amita stopped, closing her eyes as her voice broke.

"Yeah, I know," Ben said, turning back to the window. He was worried about his sister too, didn't want to think about what might be happening at the facility. They cruised on in silence for a quarter mile till Ben saw the turn. "Hey, there it is!" he called, smiling proudly at Amita.

"Congratulations," she said. Even though her voice was flat, Ben thought he saw a little smile on her face or at least, a little less of a scowl. He wasn't sure if it was a good idea coming out here, but he felt better trying to do something.

∞

'Maybe the Lightning Bug was wrong,' Chris thought, watching a human silhouette move past the curtains. He and Alex were in the dining room, their bats in hand, watching, waiting. A shadow came down the hall, moving at an unhurried pace, shoes clicking on the tile floor.

"Get ready," Alex said, putting himself in front of the kitchen.

Chris tried to stay focused, tried to keep his head in the moment, but he couldn't shake the bizarre sensation that none of this was real. It felt like the floor was dropping out from under him. He wandered past the kitchen pass-through, looking back in the window. He listened to the buzzing of wings and to Katy's footsteps hurrying away, going out the back door.

A hand pushed the cafeteria door, testing it. The door swung in and Pacheco, the security head, came in. The exit sign painted his face red as he let the door close. "How'd you get in here?" he asked.

"It was open," Alex answered.

"That's a lie, I checked these doors an hour ago, before the storm," Pacheco sneered.

Alex shrugged in response.

Pacheco looked over the room as he asked, "What are you two up to?"

"I was hungry," Alex answered.

Pacheco stared at him. "You sure have a smart mouth, don't you? Think you're the toughest guy around?" He crossed the floor, coming toward the brothers.

"No, sir," Alex said. "I know there's tougher."

Pacheco came up to Alex, his chest out, still staring. "How's your gut?" he asked, glancing down.

"Fine," Alex answered.

"Have you seen that Indian girl? Her parents were attacked earlier. We've been out looking for her." The security head leaned past Alex, looking into the kitchen.

"She's not in here," Alex said.

"No?" Pacheco asked, lifting an eyebrow.

"How could she be? Like you said the door was locked," Alex answered.

Pacheco smiled, like he heard a joke that was only for him. "Have you seen anything else? Anything strange. Something going bump in the night perhaps?"

Alex's hand tightened on the bat down by his side.

"Is she really who you're looking for?"

Pacheco glanced at the bat, tilted his head and smiled again. "I suppose not." There was a gun on his belt and his hand went down, gently touching it. He waited, watching Alex's eyes go to it. Then, while Alex's attention was on the gun, Pacheco's foot came up, smashing Alex in the chest.

Chris was in shock at seeing the way the kick lifted his brother clear off the floor. Pacheco's foot hit Alex like a truck, tossing him across the room. His bat went flying, banging on the floor with a hollow aluminum sound. A stack of cups next to the soda fountain did little to break Alex's fall as he slammed into the wall above the drink counter.

Tearing off his shirt and dropping it to the ground, Pacheco turned to Chris. In horror, Chris watched the man's body began to change. His chest split in half, as his muscles moved in a way they shouldn't. They spread apart with thick, veiny cables running between them, filling with a dark fluid.

Watching the skin change and darken to become something inhuman was the most awful thing Chris had ever seen. Then it got worse.

Pacheco's face twisted and split. His jaw dropped from his mouth, disappearing into his neck, revealing a maw full of teeth that remained disturbingly human. A long narrow tongue like a cable coiled out, whipping about. His arms lengthened with curved sickle-like blades slipping from his wrists. The worse part were the tiny pieces of human flesh left behind, the skin of his forehead, the crew cut hair or the ears that were no longer where they belonged, forced out to edges of his broad jaw.

Chris had only a moment to be afraid, to feel the shock at what he was seeing. The change was incredibly fast, and before it was even complete, Pacheco launched himself. The security head landed on Chris, pinning him to the ground. It was only by luck that Chris got his bat up and held it in a perfect bunting position while the weight of the monster pushed against him, crushing him against the floor. The curved blades rested on the bat, their razor edges slicing into the soft aluminum, slowly going through it.

Struggling to push up, Chris stared into Pacheco's open mouth. The creature seemed to be smiling at him as its tongue worked its way towards him. The narrow appendage was striated with muscle and black, goofilled tubing. There was a sharp, needle-like point at the tongue's tip, which dripped with venom as it twisted back like a cobra ready to strike.

Alex coughed, rolling off the counter, spitting blood. He was hurt bad. On his hands and knees, he struggled to get up and resisted the urge to pass out or collapse completely.

He saw Chris pinned down with that thing on top of him and forced himself to his feet, using the counter for support. He grabbed the closest thing he could find, a coffee carafe, and tossed it at Pacheco's back. The glass shattered but didn't cause any damage. Still, it gave Chris a moment while the creature turned and looked at Alex. The tongue was whipping around its mouth as if Pacheco wanted to strike Alex from across the room.

Alex struggled over to a chair, lifted it over his head, and tossed it at the monster. Watching, Pacheco laughed a little as it bounced off him, entertained by the young man's struggle. Alex was just barely able to stand, but he was still trying to fight.

Pacheco looked like a cat toying with mice. He'd been human once and as such he still remembered what pleasure was, and this was the closest to joy he'd felt since being joined with the alien tech that made him so powerful.

Chris tried to focus, knowing he only had a second before Pacheco would bury the stinger in him. He watched the tongue dance from the monster's mouth and start to coil. An idea entered his head that he immediately hated. Unfortunately, he didn't see many other options.

Chris let go of his bat. It fell on his chest with the blades still half buried in it. The creature's weight slammed down, pressing hard into his ribs. He wondered if his bones would break as he reached out grabbing the coiled tongue. It was icy cold in his grasp, a chemical feeling of numbness laced through him, but Chris wouldn't let go. He pulled at it as Pacheco twisted his head, trying to tug himself away.

Chris still didn't let go. He held as tightly as he could to the appendage as Pacheco roared in rage. The monster got to his feet, lifting Chris from the floor.

Alex watched from the corner of his eye, as he searched around for his bat. Finding it beneath a table, he picked it up and rushed Pacheco with it held high. He swung down as hard as he could on the monster's head and saw the creature shiver with the force. The blow rang through Pacheco's skull. Chris could feel it in his hands, still holding the tongue. A bladed arm came up swinging back at Alex, trying to cut him in half, but Alex half-ducked, half-fell back behind a table, knocking it over.

Feeling his feet dragged across the floor, Chris stayed in tight, too close for Pacheco to use his blades. Instead, the creature's hands tried to go around his neck, but Chris blocked him with his elbows, holding them high. Then Pacheco's hands closed on his torso.

The monster twisted and swung his whole body, using his massive neck muscles to try and shake Chris loose, which sent him flying through the air, but he never let go of the tongue. It broke away in his hands, coming off like a bee's stinger.

As he smashed into a wall, Chris heard the creature scream in pain. He looked back to see black fluid leaking from its mouth as its eyes narrowed, staring at him.

Pacheco bent down, ready to pounce on Chris and bury his blades in him. But as the monster pulled back, ready to leap, Alex took the table he'd fallen behind and used it like a battering ram, charging forward, slamming into the monster and knocking it off its feet.

The blades swung out, slashing through the plywood and veneer. It just barely missed Alex.

"I should've killed you!" Pacheco screamed, throwing off the pieces of the table. Alex tripped as he back-peddled away, going down under legs that were losing strength.

Pacheco, the hunter, stood over him, raising its blades high again. But before it could drop them and cut Alex in two, something jabbed it's back. Pacheco felt a strange sensation, the icy rush of numbing poison.

The hunter had left behind most of the weaknesses of its human form. Its skin, its true skin, was incredibly tough. It'd been designed that way by his creators. Turning in surprise, he reached back, feeling for the thing that had somehow made its way through his hide, and found his own stinger.

His body began to react immediately. Countermeasures to his venom were released into what passed for his bloodstream, trying to purge the venom before it forced him into shut down. It was excruciating. Pacheco screamed in absolute rage, twisting back to grab for the stinger.

Chris watched it tearing at its own flesh and saw his brother too close, beneath the monster. He ducked down, grabbed Alex by an arm, and pulled him away. The bladed arms were swinging wildly, but Chris stayed low, moving fast to wrap his arms around his brother's chest, dragging him back. Blood seeped through Alex's T-shirt and left a slick mark across the floor.

Banging through the kitchen door, breathing hard, Chris didn't have time to look up to see where the creature was, but he could hear it roaring. As the door closed behind him, the roaring stopped. Chris moved fast dropping his brother out of the way and going to push one of the serving stations behind the door, wedging it against a countertop.

Only a moment later there was a loud crash as Pacheco barreled into the door, which opened a few inches before hitting the serving station. The monster charged into it again, then slashed with his blades, cleaving a clean triangle from the door's top corner.

Chris picked up his brother, worried that Alex wasn't saying anything. He'd gone limp. Chris dragged him back past the stoves, down the hall where they'd found the Lightning Bug, not sure what he'd do from there. Maybe hide in the pantry or the freezer or try to get outside. He didn't know how far he was going to be able to go while dragging Alex, but he knew he wasn't going to leave his brother here.

He looked around the corner, back at the door, expecting to see it explode in or torn to pieces, but the opening had gone quiet. Then Chris considered the kitchen pass-through. It wasn't a large opening, but it was probably big enough for the creature to get in.

A magnetic block on the counter near him was full of butcher knives. Carefully, Chris lowered his brother to the floor and took two of the blades, struggling to grip them with his numb hands. Then he hid around the corner, next to Alex, waiting for the creature to come for them.

# Chapter Thirty-One

A few minutes after taking the turn, Ben started to recognize the rocky landscape. He breathed out a sigh of relief as the canyon walls rose on either side of the little pick-up truck. In sunlight, Ben had felt small enough under these cliffs, but in the dark, they were a different landscape, more claustrophobic. Ben felt as if he and Amita were descending into another world not meant for humans.

He kept his foot on the accelerator, already feeling the tires slipping. He thought he was in four-wheel drive, but he wasn't sure. There was a lever in the center of the floor with four choices. Two of them had 4x4 printed next to them, so it was a little confusing.

Despite what he'd told Amita he'd only ever driven his aunt's station wagon once and that had been on a dare. He'd driven to a friend's house to pick up a bunch of kids from school. None of them liked him, including his friend, but they were willing to put up with him as long as he was willing to chauffeur them around. After they went to a couple of stores in his neighborhood, someone came up with the idea of going to Coronado Island. Then Ben pulled onto Route 5 and quickly realized, while trying to merge, that the highway was too much for him.

He'd lost his nerve and taken the very next exit. He had to find his way home on back roads with a car full of kids making fun of him. Ben had tried to ignore them. He'd learned a long time ago that if he smiled along with the jokes people made about him, then he could fit in a little. It still hurt when people picked on him, but at least he wasn't lonely.

"Nice job," Amita said when they saw the cliffs. Ben just nodded, not wanting her to know how scared he was and feeling the truck struggle through the sandy soil.

They drove on in silence till they could see where the opening to the slot canyon was hidden. Fifty yards out Ben felt his tires bog down in the sand. He was still gunning the engine, but with every spin, the tires sunk deeper into the ground. He tried putting the truck in reverse. Then he tried turning the wheel left and right. That only buried them deeper. "Looks like we're walking from here," he said, turning to Amita.

They climbed out of the truck and followed the beam of the headlights like a shining path toward the crack in the cliff face. This was the very spot that Jake had brought them in the afternoon.

Amita had sworn then that the creature inside had no intention of hurting them. She still believed that, but as they crossed into the dark, she had to admit she was a little scared.

The headlights shone into the canyon's entrance, but they didn't travel far, only enough to see the floor shimmer a little, reflecting off a pool of water. The monsoon had come and gone, but the soil hadn't had time to absorb all that rain. Ben and Amita turned a corner and found themselves out of the headlight's glow in complete darkness.

Amita placed her hand on the wall and stepped forward. Her feet moved slowly while water seeped into her shoes. It was incredibly cold. The water rose to her shins as she continued on.

"It looks so different in the dark. I'm not sure I'll be able to see where I turned before." Amita said while looking toward the sky. The clouds were moving off, letting starlight through, but it didn't help much so deep in the canyon. "Maybe you should lead the way. You said you've got that whole sense of direction thing, right?"

"It only works when I can see where I'm going," he answered.

"Try what I'm doing. Keep your hand on the wall."

Ben nodded. Of course, Amita couldn't see it, but she felt him step around her and reach out. Ben closed his eyes and tried to remember how the space looked in daylight. Amita hadn't gone far into the canyon earlier. The turn she'd taken was almost at the exit.

"Maybe you should hold onto my shoulder or something, so no matter what, we don't get separated," he said.

Amita reached up and touched his arm, which was still wet from the rain earlier, but it was warmer than the cliff wall. She could tell that Ben was shivering a little from standing in the cold water. "Here we go," he said moving forward.

Their steps were slow and careful. When Ben reached a spot where the wall began to turn, he followed it, not remembering any branches before the passage they'd found Amita in. He was almost certain this was the way. They continued in silence, neither of them wanting to talk about the growing problem they both sensed. The water was getting deeper.

There had been so much rain coming through the canyon in the last few hours that some of it had stayed behind, too much for the soil to take. The sand under them was loose, making Ben's feet sink into it. With every step, it was getting harder and harder to walk. At one point the suction was so strong it pulled his shoe off.

He reached below the surface to find it, but the sneaker had disappeared completely.

"We keep going this way, and we'll have to start swimming soon," he said, feeling the water touch his waist and soaking through his jeans.

Amita was still looking toward the top of the canyon. The night was bright enough for her to tell where the canyon walls ended and even make out a few shadowy details near the ledge. She was trying to find the place where she'd seen the glass diamond. This time though, there was no reflection to catch her attention.

"We must be getting close," she said, but Ben didn't answer till she added, "Right?"

"I don't know," he admitted. The water wasn't getting any deeper, but the sand was. The struggle to move forward became more and more tiring for him. He felt the soupy soil swallow his leg up to his knee. Then he pushed his other leg down to try and free it, feeling that leg become stuck too.

"Hang on a second," he called as he pulled away from her, bending at the waist to attempt to pull himself out with a half-panicked breaststroke. His legs didn't budge. In fact, they sunk further.

Amita reached her hand out to find his shoulder. It was much lower than she expected. "You're getting deeper," she said.

"I know," Ben responded while his hand searched the wall, trying to find anything to grab onto.

He felt Amita reach under his arms. "NO! Don't — " he yelled, but it was too late. She pulled up with all her strength. The effort pushed her down into the muck too.

Amita felt the sand compress her pants against her legs as her own force drove her down into the soil. She was in sand up to her waist while the icy cold water was at her chest. "That wasn't a good idea," she admitted.

"You think?" Ben attempted to turn toward her. As he did, he felt himself sink deeper. Then he tried turning back towards the wall, still searching for a handhold and finding only smooth rock.

"Stop moving!" Amita shouted at him.

"I'm stopped! I'm stopped" Ben yelled back, holding his hands up. After a moment's pause, he said into the dark, "So now what?"

"Hypothermia, probably," Amita answered, feeling her body start to shake. Her teeth were chattering.

Ben reached his hand out in the dark trying to find Amita's. He found her forearm and followed it down to close his fingers around hers. He was just about to say something reassuring when Amita opened her mouth and screamed at the top of her lungs, "HELP! Please help!"

Ben never knew she had such a loud voice. "Warn someone before you do that," he said.

Amita paused for a moment. "We're not getting out of this on our own. You need to start yelling too," she said as she started calling out again.

"Help!" Ben called once, then stopped. He saw something up at the top of canyon.

Against the gray of the sky, there was a dark form, bounding between the cliff walls, coming toward them. "Look," he said, pointing to the thing.

Amita stopped yelling and watched it pause just above Ben, a massive black spot. Ben could smell the thing. The odor reminded him of a pet rabbit he once had. He tried to find its eyes, but in the dark all he could see was a black void hanging from the cliff wall. Its mouth opened and he could feel warm air, sense the faint odor of chewed plants, grass and roots.

"You're the one, the boy that threw a rock at me?" the creature asked in a voice that rumbled through him.

Ben had almost forgotten about that. He thought back for a moment, remembering how he had beamed a stone right off the creature's head. "Yeah, that was me. Um, Sorry about that," he said. There was an awkward silence in which Ben could sense the thing staring at him.

Amita asked, "We're stuck. We were coming to find you, then the sand got a hold of us. Do you think you could help us out?"

"Yes," it answered simply. Then with a quick motion, it brought its head down to Ben, opened its mouth and closed its jaws around him, swallowing the top of the boy's head. Ben felt the beak-like opening envelop him, burying him in that vegetable smell and covering his eyes with a thin coating of mucus.

He struggled as the creature pulled him. He yelled. His mouth was the only part of him uncovered, but when he opened it, alien saliva dripped past his lips, gagging him.

A loud sucking sound echoed though the canyon as his legs were pulled free of the sand and water. Carefully, the creature brought him to dry ground, dropping him on a pile of sand that had been banked up by the water. Ben flopped down on his butt, trying to wipe the mucus from his face.

He watched the creature move back to Amita, its clawed feet and hands keeping it attached to the walls. One long arm reached out to her, and Amita took it willingly. She stretched up till the creature could wrap its entire arm around her. He gently pulled her free, then turned and carried her back to Ben.

Ben was still having a hard time seeing. One, because of the saliva, and two, because it was so dark. Still, he saw the creature's handling of Amita clear enough.

"Hey, how come you didn't use your mouth on her?" Ben asked.

"Because she didn't throw a rock at me," the creature answered honestly.

# Chapter thirty-Two

Chris wasn't sure how much time had passed, how long he'd been crouched down in the kitchen with a knife in each hand, waiting for Pacheco, for that monster, to come for them. Seconds felt like hours. He felt the muscles in his legs tighten as his brother moaned next to him. Alex was bleeding so much. 'The wound on his stomach must've torn back open,' Chris thought, knowing he had to do something.

He looked around the kitchen and saw a stack of neatly folded linens. His eyes stayed on the passthrough as he shuffled over to them. The red light of an exit sign shone down on the mostly dark cafeteria, while the kitchen was lit by coolers that seemed too bright. Chris stared at the broad opening of the passthrough, not sure if Pacheco was out there waiting in the shadows. 'He could be standing right there, staring at me and I'd never know it,' Chris thought, remembering how dark the monster's skin was, the way it seemed to absorb the light.

He thought he'd heard it leave a moment before, when it sounded like the cafeteria door had opened and closed, but that could be a trick. Chris stood slowly, staring out. He was breathing too loudly. He was tempted to get a better look by stepping toward the window pass-through, but first, he took the linens to his brother.

The blood from Alex's stomach was spilling onto the floor, forming a puddle. It looked like a lot. Chris lifted the t-shirt away, and in the low lights, the wound was a darker spot, sticky and wet. He held a few towels tight against his brother's belly. "Oh, god," Chris muttered softly, feeling a different kind of fear.

"What, what is it?" Alex mumbled while his eyes tried to flutter open.

"Shh," Chris said. "I don't know if it's gone."

Alex was quiet for a moment. When he spoke again, his voice was pained. "It was Pacheco? This whole time it was him?"

"We should've known that guy was evil," Chris said.

Alex's eyes went to the pass-through. "Sounds quiet out there." He tried to get up, grimacing with the effort.

Chris kept his hand tight on his brother's belly.

"Go easy. You're hurt pretty bad."

Alex stared down. "Looks like I popped a stitch," he settled back on the wall and glanced again toward the cafeteria. "It's probably gone."

"Yeah, I know, I just haven't looked yet." Chris placed Alex's hand over the wound. "Hold this," he said, starting toward the window.

"Careful," Alex said behind him.

Chris nodded and put his head out far enough to see, hoping that it wasn't about to be ripped off. He scanned the room. It was empty.

"It's gone."

"Maybe . . . but you know it's not done. It's going to go after her."

Chris turned around to face his brother. Alex was using the wall, forcing himself to his feet. He leaned back as he struggled to take off his t-shirt.

"What are you doing?" Chris asked, coming over to help.

Alex pushed the bloody shirt towards him. "Here, tear this in half, right down the middle."

Chris did, then his brother said, "Tie it around me, tight." He motioned to his stomach.

"Alex, what the hell? You need to sit down while I get help."

Alex shook his head. Everywhere his hand went, he left a bloody print. His words were short and choppy. "It wants that bug thing . . . It's going after Katy. We've got to stop it."

# Chapter Thirty-Three

Outside, while the rain was still falling, Dr. Virtanen drove down one of the broken dirt paths that passed for a road at the facility. His wipers could barely keep up as the heart of the storm passed overhead.

The scientist had just come from the observatory, from the event horizon of the thing he'd created, the thing that he might have to destroy if the power wasn't restored. The nature of Virtanen's work required isolation. His investors had paid an ungodly amount to run lines out to this remote plateau, but now a storm was close to ruining it.

He glanced back at the observatory, thinking of the years he'd spent bringing this project together, lining up men with vision, and money, all to create something truly amazing. 'He should still be there,' he thought, looking back at the white dome again.

He should be standing by, ready to throw the switch. There were protocols in place, safeties for when the power went out. The second device was ready. He'd made certain of that. Sitting on temporary staging in front of the event horizon, it only required him to activate it.

He thought of the Patels, lying in the street in front of his house. Their discovery of a certain kind of exotic matter was what had finally made this all possible. Together they had built a device that directed a nuclear explosion into a plasma suspension field that held a subatomic wormhole.

The plasma chamber alone had taken up nearly all the space in the observatory, enough mechanisms to create a point that was trillions of degrees hotter than the air around it. That hot point of superheated plasma was a state of matter that only ever existed in a lab or at the moment of the big bang. It was a space smaller than a human cell, but it was enough to feed their wormhole, a tiny, temporary hole in the quantum foam of a single atom.

They'd detected the wormhole using Dr. Johnson's theories, theories that'd barely been proven before being absorbed and classified by the US government.

Those ideas, created by Dr. Virtanen and Dr. Johnson working together nearly two decades ago, had been declared a matter of national security, applied to stealth tech and black book weapon systems. There were rumors of soldiers who could side-step reality and walk-through walls. Of course, that had to be a rumor.

Dr. Virtanen and Dr. Johnson were never allowed to publish their discoveries. Any reports they'd made were redacted and filed away, but that hadn't stopped Dr. Virtanen from using the techniques they'd devised to find a wormhole here in the desert or more specifically to predict the appearance of one.

Wormholes were extremely short-lived events.

The night they'd done it, the night they'd thrown the switch, Dr. Virtanen had been elated. The energy released had been astounding. In a flash of light, all the machinery for forty meters around the event had dissolved, leaving a hole in space, an estimated two meters around, floating beneath the observatory's dome. It glowed and hummed, wanting to expand. Only a grid of magnetic plates, fed a constant flow of electricity, held it in place.

That should've been the exciting time. That should've been the moment when they got to perform real science. They should've been able to begin observing what they created, to understand what it was and what was on the other side. Instead, something went wrong.

There was a burst of radio waves, noisy radiation blasting out that blinded most of the electronic observing devices. Then something solid came through that exited into the chamber, a glowing ball of light. Some of the scientists thought they might have seen wings on it, but it was glowing too brightly to make out details.

One thing was certain. This was a life form or at least sentient. It moved toward them in a way that seemed to be a type of communication, repeating patterns. Excitement had filled the observation room as they watched it float around like a glowing butterfly, coming toward them, toward the blast shields that were in the process of lowering. This was the moment of contact, the greatest moment in the pursuit of science. But then something else came through.

Moving fast, the second being shot from the void and blasted into the roof of the observatory. Much larger than the creature that'd come through first, this new thing had cracked the dome apart and took off into the night sky. The first creature, the smaller one, was caught in some sort of energy wake and was dragged out of the opening as well.

In the observation booth, the scientists stared at each other, not sure what to say. Dr. Virtanen had immediately ordered the power be increased to the magnetic plates, hoping to keep the field stable. Their displays no longer worked, but as he stared at the void, he was certain it was growing.

He couldn't take his eyes away from the bizarre light show that seemed to exist and not exist, pulsing and folding in on itself like a living thing. At that moment something else came through. The entity followed a course close to the first large object, but not exactly the same, hitting the dome and making the opening a little larger. The power to the magnetic plates fluctuated.

Virtanen's eyes were on the wormhole, this time he was certain he saw it grow, nearly doubling in size. "More power, increase the field!" he called as in the moment he realized how dangerous what they made could be. How fast it could grow. The wormhole was feeding on the matter around it, absorbing it from the very air. There had been theories that this was possible, but they hadn't been sure. Still, they'd built the magnetic bubble hoping to stabilize the opening's size, which worked as long as the grid stayed together.

He watched in near panic, hoping nothing else would come through, that there would be no other objects or aliens or whatever else tearing the dome's metal walls apart. For five days there hadn't been another incident, the wormhole had stayed the same size. Nothing else came through, but the things that were already here started to cause trouble.

He thought of the Patels again. They'd been his friends for years, partners in what he'd created here, now they were as cold as ice, sitting on a slab. He hoped they could find some way to help them, and that their daughter was okay. He'd be out looking for her himself, but first, he wanted to check on the generators. They were the only source of power feeding the observatory now. If they failed for any reason, then all of this would be over. He'd have to throw the switch on the device sitting in front of the wormhole.

But if he used the second device, that would be it. He'd never get funding again. He'd spend the rest of his career pouring over old data. After he published, someone else would follow in his footsteps. They'd do it better, safer, and he would be a footnote in their papers. That's if the secondary device even worked. The wormhole had proven capable of absorbing massive amounts of energy, he wasn't sure if the directed nuclear explosion would be enough to close it. He didn't want to imagine what would happen if it wasn't.

He pulled his pickup into the garage at the generator building, happy to hear them humming away. Jake Bizahalone came out of the heavy steel door that led to the generators and down a short flight of steps from the loading dock. As he approached Virtanen, he pulled away the ear protection he'd been wearing.

"How are they running?" Virtanen asked, getting out of the truck.

Jake looked tired. His steps didn't have their usual bounce. His easy smile was gone. "Just fine. I've got one going and a second one warmed up in reserve, in an hour I'll cycle the other two in. There's plenty of fuel, enough to run for a month."

"Hopefully, we won't need them for that long. I've already sent men out to inspect the lines to see if they can find the break."

"That may not be safe in this weather," Jake pointed out, turning to look at the rain spraying in, soaking the concrete floor.

"It's got to be done," Virtanen said, walking toward the door. He picked up another set of protective earphones hanging nearby.

Jake followed behind. "I've got to talk to you about what I saw in that canyon. I'm fairly certain it ain't from around here. Least I've never seen anything like it. I asked Pacheco what he was doing about it, but all he did was ask more questions."

Virtanen looked back from halfway up the steps. "Look, Jake, I'm aware of the situation. We're working on it. That's the whole reason Pacheco was transferred here."

He lifted the earphones to his head, but Jake put his hand out stopping him. "He's barely done anything outside of interrogating me and the kids. Do you guys even know what these things are?"

Virtanen pulled the earphones away. "Look, we're working on it, but this whole discussion is above your pay grade."

Jake had spent most of the night in the security office, answering questions but not getting any information in return. His patience was at an end. "'My pay grade?' Man, that thing out there was bigger than a bear, and it came from this place. I've got family out there to worry about. The thing landed on my uncle's farm." Jake came closer, his voice turning cold. "You're seriously going to talk to me about my pay grade?"

Virtanen felt his temper growing as well. "You listen to me—" he began, pointing his finger into Jake's chest, but then he stopped, hearing someone call him.

He recognized his daughter's voice above the wind. "Dad, help!"

Turning towards the garage doors, he struggled to see her through the storm, past the glare of the garage lights. She was moving fast, occasionally looking over her shoulder with a bundle in her arms.

Katy came out of the rain, crossed into the garage and ran to him. "Dad, you gotta help," she said, attempting to catch her breath, "you gotta listen."

Her father was still angry, but in spite of that, he noticed that his daughter was soaking wet. "What are you doing?" he asked, shaking his head. "Why are you running out in the rain like a lunatic?"

Katy glanced back the way she came. "I've got to tell you, but not here," she said. "We need to get somewhere safe." She wasn't sure, but she thought she saw someone moving in the storm, coming from the cafeteria.

"What? Why?" Virtanen demanded.

"Let's just go inside," Katy began.

Then another voice added, "We have much to discuss."

Virtanen and Jake both looked down at the bundle in Katy's arms. That's where the voice came from. A face that was nowhere near human looked back at them. Virtanen stared at it, stepping away. "What is that?" he asked Katy.

"It's complicated, but it needs to talk to you, Dad," Katy said. She noticed Jake glancing out into the storm and turned her head to see what was there.

A single form was approaching through the rain. For a moment she was hopeful that it would be Chris or Alex, but the person was too tall. She recognized the muscular form of Pacheco. As he came closer to the lights, Katy saw that his clothes were disheveled and that he was in the middle of trying to button his shirt.

"We need to get inside," Katy said, darting towards the door, going up the stairs past her father.

"What's the matter with you?" Virtanen asked, stepping into Pacheco's path.

Pacheco's face was pale, twisted, and stern. He looked like he was in pain, walking with a slight limp and there was something oozing from the side of his mouth. Virtanen thought it was blood, but it looked too dark, more like motor oil.

"What's going on here?" Virtanen asked.

"Sir —Your daughter — she is putting — she is putting this whole project at risk," Pacheco said as more black goo dribbled from his mouth. His voice sounded terrible, like a chainsaw struggling to keep from stalling.

Virtanen stopped in his tracks, staring at him.

"What's wrong with you?"

Jake had moved up onto the loading dock closer to Katy. He never took his eyes off Pacheco, seeing something was terribly wrong with him.

Pacheco watched Jake, then looked down at his uniform, which had become soaked in the black fluid. He glanced back at Virtanen, "Forget this," he mumbled, tearing his shirt off. His body changed quickly, spreading and twisting, his torso coming apart and his face seeming to break as his jaw spread, spraying the fluid over Virtanen.

While his blades extended, he shoved Virtanen, tossing him across the garage. His hands lengthened. While his legs popped and changed. Then he swooped forward with a few wide steps, charging toward Katy.

"Get the hell out of here," Jake ordered, jabbing in the door code, pulling it open, and shoving her through. He slammed the door behind Katy.

Jake watched in horror as the thing that had once been the head of security came at him. He had only a moment to pick up a piece of pipe that'd been lying by the door and to hold it up in defense.

Listening on the other side, Katy found a large slide bolt and slapped it shut as something slammed into the door. She heard Jake grunt. "Oh, god," she moaned. That's when a long blade came thrusting through, nearly skewering her.

Katy backed away as another blade pierced the steel. The blades retracted, then came again and again, quickly tearing the door apart. Katy glanced down at the alien in her arms.

"We need to hide," she said, turning to run, looking for any place the monster wouldn't find them. in the large open space filled with the sound of running generators.

## Chapter Thirty-Four

The creature next to Amita was a dark spot towering above her. She had so many questions but couldn't get the words out because her teeth wouldn't stop chattering.

"So, you got a name?" Ben asked. He had stopped acting upset about being in the creature's mouth, though he had gone back to the pool twice to use the icy ground water to wipe the saliva off.

The creature's voice came out slowly, each word considered. "My true name is very long, but you may call me Tearmai. I am a Drake."

"Cool," said Ben before turning to his shivering friend.

"We've got to get you warm," he said reaching out and touching Amita's shoulders. He rubbed his hands up and down on her arms, trying to make friction.

They sensed the Drake moving to the canyon wall. As he smashed his fist into it, fragments flew in the air and rocks tumbled, hitting the ground.

"Whoa!" Ben said, jumping back from the rubble.

Tearmai pushed the pieces together with his foot, then held something up. "Cover your eyes," he said. Ben and Amita turned away, putting their hands over their faces, then heard a spark followed by a bright flare.

When they slowly took those hands away, they saw Tearmai holding a painfully bright torch. Despite the discomfort, Ben and Amita watched the creature in fascination. Ben hadn't gotten a very good look at Tearmai before. He only remembered his size. Now, in the light from the torch, he could see the long thick arms, the armor plating with tiny spikes and its deep sad eyes.

The creature moved down to point the torch at the pile of rocks. Quickly they began to glow and throw off heat. Tearmai turned the torch down so that its white flame became a duller orange. Then he motioned to the hot rocks. "Please come get warm."

Ben and Amita sat down, crossing their legs and holding their arms out over the warm stones, and looked up at the massive Drake. He crossed his legs leaving the torch lit so they could see him.

"We came to ask you for help. Something is here. It's hurting people, stinging them. It hurt my parents," Amita said.

"Yes, the Hunter is close to my friend. He's scared." Tearmai motioned to his head.

"You can tell that from here?" Ben asked.

Tearmai starred at Ben as if he didn't understand the question. After a moment he nodded, a thought occurring. "My friend's species can touch minds. I feel his fear," he explained.

Ben and Amita glanced at each other before Ben continued, "He asked us to help him escape. My sister and these two other guys are going to do what they can for your friend, but that other thing is still out there."

"They are going to help?" The Drake tilted his head quizzically.

"Um, yeah," Ben said. "That Hunter is hurting people. We want to stop it."

Tearmai nodded slowly again.

"Can you stop it, the Hunter? Can you fight it?" Amita asked.

"It is strong, dangerous, made for this. I am strong, but not really dangerous. Still, I will do what I can. I came to stop it, to take them all back. What happens here . . . It happens," the Drake explained.

Ben tried to understand what the creature meant. Looking at him, he wondered how he could think of himself as not being dangerous. He looked built for battle with a hulking body and a face that reminded him of a dragon from a fantasy game. Ben stared at his mouth and for a moment wondered how exactly his head had fit in there.

"What about the people who are already hurt?" Amita asked. "Can you help them?"

Tearmai was quiet for a moment, staring at her, "I want to help everyone," he said, then went silent, still staring. He looked away before speaking again. "Perhaps my friend, the Lightning Bug can help . . . But I don't know. . . We all must leave, none of us belong here, but my vessel is damaged." He pointed up the canyon wall, where his diamond vessel sat. "It is the only way I can cross the void safely, but it has no more propulsion. No way to get it to the void and it is very heavy, even for me."

"Well, we have a truck, a pick-up. It could carry your ship. It's big enough, right?" Ben asked, looking at Amita.

"Maybe," Amita said, "but it's stuck in the sand."

The Drake stood up. "I'll just have to unstuck it."

# Chapter Thirty-Five

The machines were incredibly loud, but not so loud that Katy couldn't hear the door being hacked to pieces behind her. A smacking sound followed high pitched rips as the metal tore apart. She thought about her father and Jake as she hurried back toward the generators. 'Were they alright? How bad had that thing hurt them,' she wondered, feeling awful. She didn't want to think that her father might be dead. She'd been so mad at him, but now imagining him gone nearly broke her heart. And Jake, he was one of the nicest guys she'd met here. Always smiling, always friendly. 'He didn't deserve this.'

Everyone had agreed to try and save the alien, but somehow Katy felt responsible, as if it'd been her idea alone. She thought of Chris and Alex, adding up the count of people who were hurt, all because of that decision, all because of this thing, she thought looking down at the Lightening Bug in her arms. For a moment she wanted to put it down and give up, find a corner to hide in, while these creatures finished their little game. The diesel generators fired their pistons, pumping so fast that they formed a heavy thrumming that vibrated through Katy, making it hard to think. 'All that power,' Katy wondered, 'and it was for one purpose. To control what her father made.' She glanced at the alien again and knew she had to keep going.

She moved past an office and the employee lockers, coming out into a space similar to a warehouse. Laid out across the floor, four generators stood in a row, bigger than most pick-up trucks. A catwalk ran overhead fifteen feet in the air and massive banks of gray electrical boxes covered every wall. The space was wide open with very few places to hide under banks of glowing industrial lights.

She felt the Lightning Bug against her chest and knew that her heart was beating against Brash's body as she looked for another exit, any way to escape. There was a room to her right, a large entrance way, and a dark space beyond.

Quickly she went there, her hand searching over the cinderblock wall for a switch. When she finally turned on the light banks, she saw a tool room with work benches and neatly organized bins of spare parts. There were a few more lockers, but she couldn't stand the thought of trying to hide in one of those. She didn't like the idea of waiting for that creature to come and find her. In the distance, she could still hear the slashing.

She saw rubber mallets but passed them by. Her hand ran over the bench and stopped when she felt a heavy wrench. Transferring Brash to one arm, she picked up the tool, swinging it a little wondering if hitting the monster would do anything.

The work bench ran seven meters, the whole length of the room. Just before the far wall were two entrances on either side. Katy rushed to them. To the left was a short flight of concrete stairs going down to a door. To her right going up were stairs made of metal grates, the kind you could see through.

She went down the concrete ones, but then stopped. The four steps ended at a landing and a door that seemed too short. In large black letters was a warning, "DANGER HIGH VOLTAGE," with lightning images painted in yellow. Her eyes went back to the high wall which kept going up past the hanging light fixtures. Massive wires, hidden inside heavy conduit came down it secured to the cinderblocks following the metal stairs. Smaller cables joined the larger ones. All of them ending at this door, disappearing into the wall just above it.

"That leads to the observatory," Brash said, nodding towards the door.

"How do you know?" Katy whispered.

"All the power goes there. We should follow it."

Trying to ignore the warning, Katy reached for the heavy handle and pulled it open revealing a long cement passage less than five feet tall. Pipes housing the heavy wires, covered the walls and ceiling. Only the floor was clear.

The tunnel was dark. Katy looked around trying to find a switch, but there was none. She pictured being trapped in there, the creature catching up to her and running her down "I don't want to go that way."

She glanced back towards the stairs. That's when she heard metal dragging in the generator room. The Hunter had made it through the door. It was scratching the ground loudly with its blades as it stalked her. "Come out, come out wherever you are," it called with Pacheco's voice.

Katy left the door to the electrical passage open, turned and started running, going up the concrete steps, then the metal ones before Brash had time to complain. The noise from the generators would've covered the sound anyway. Reaching the top, she looked down trying to understand where she was and saw the catwalk run over the generator room in front of her.

The metal walkway ran the length of the room, straight over each generator. It only turned once to an offshoot that went out to the massive diesel tanks behind the building. Large casement windows covered the back wall, but in the middle was a door. 'There's my exit,' Katy thought, starting to run. She was halfway down the walkway when she stopped abruptly. Her eyes went to the floor and her body tightened in fear.

The Hunter was below her. The creature was stalking slowly next to the generators.

A few nights before, out in the desert, she'd seen this thing attack her friend. It'd been a shadow then, its skin not reflecting the stars or the moon. Here, though, she could see it clearly, all the horror of a human body twisted into a half-animal hunting machine. She remembered that sketch she'd done of it and now knew that she'd missed so many details, but she also knew she'd never go back to her drawing, even if this thing haunted her nightmares.

Frozen. Unable to run. Watching it move deliberately, she knew it was tracking her. He was leaving a trail of oily, dark fluid across the floor.

She looked at its face and remembered his eyes in the interrogation room. Pacheco had dark eyes, but those eyes were gone now, replaced by things that were black and glassy like a shark's.

Katy took a step forward, hoping the sound from the generators would cover her footfalls. She tried to judge the distance to the back door but struggled to look away from the monster. One cautious step followed another. She felt certain she was making too much noise.

Glancing at the door to the diesel tanks, Katy couldn't believe how far it was. It'd seemed so close before. It'd seemed like freedom. She looked back over her shoulder, back towards the stairs, thinking of the little door with its warning signs.

'Would that way have been faster? How long would I be in the dark, in that tunnel,' she wondered.

Katy didn't want to find out. She'd go for the back door where the diesel tanks were. Another step turned her attention back to the exit. Her eyes went to the floor, looking for the creature. Empty.

The black trail ended, but the Hunter was nowhere to be found. Katy's heart raced. Then her eyes fell on the generators, the third in the row. The creature was there, on top of it, crouched down, its bizarre head moving slowly, surveying the room.

Katy tried not to move. She held her breath staring, watching the inhuman eyes turn towards her.

The catwalk was shadowy. The lights, most of which were off, shone on the machinery, not on this access way and Katy hoped it was dark enough that the Hunter wouldn't see her. Its eyes turned till they fell on her. His head stopped; the black orbs focused in.

Before Katy could even think about running, the Hunter took a single leap, bounding high and clearing the catwalk's handrail. Its feet slammed down onto the metal walkway, making it vibrate beneath her feet.

Pacheco, the Hunter, stood in her way, blocking the exit. She felt Brash in her arms, felt his entire body tremble and knew he was just as terrified as she was.

## Chapter Thirty-Six

Ben was holding up the alien torch, occasionally swinging it around like a sword. "Well, at least he left us the light."

Amita stared at him in annoyance as they stood at the entrance to the canyon. "Do you have to play with that thing?"

Tearmai had led them outside a few minutes before, going back for his ship.

"I'm not playing with it. I'm just checking it out," Ben said, holding the flame to the rock face, which soon began to heat up and glow. "How hot do you think it gets?"

"Really hot," Amita said, stepping back into the canyon's entrance. She could hear the Drake coming. He was grunting with the effort of dragging his ship. Amita grabbed the torch from Ben's hand, pointing it back toward the sound.

"Hey—" Ben started to say but stopped when he saw the diamond come slowly out of the dark. It was the size of a car. The light from the torch seemed to dance over its triangle panels, running like mercury. It lay across Tearmai's shoulders while his face twisted with the effort.

Ben looked back at their truck, stuck in the sand, then leaned toward Amita whispering, "How are we going to get that back?"

Amita shrugged in response. There wasn't much room at the canyon entrance, so the pair had to move as Tearmai stomped toward them. The diamond squeezed past the walls, and the Drake continued slowly toward the truck. He lowered the ship to the sand.

Out in the open, the alien seemed even larger. He was almost as wide as the tailgate. After bending down and looking at the tires buried in the sand, he grunted, grabbed the bumper and pulled, lifting the back end into the air. The truck bounced on its springs when he dropped it to the ground

Ben sidled up next to the Drake. "Actually, if you want to turn the whole thing around and point us that way," he suggested, motioning up the trail.

Tearmai's eyes were incredibly human, asking Ben if he were serious.

"It'll make it quicker getting out of here. Less chance of getting stuck," Ben added.

Tearmai nodded, then bent down, lifting the pickup again and started to turn it completely around. The front wheels made large circles in the sand as a deep sound rumbled in the creature's chest and puffed out his beak. Through the effort, he managed to say in his slow cadence, "I can sense my friend . . . Very frightened. The Hunter almost has him. . . He's going to destroy him."

"What about my sister? Do you know what's happening to her?" Ben asked, jumping out of Tearmai's way. The truck was still in the air.

Amita pulled Ben back even further as the vehicle bounced on the ground. "Hopefully, it will only sting her," the Drake said. "Everyone up there," he motioned toward the facility, "It's impossible to know who they are. The monster was given a mission. Its master won't risk causality," Tearmai motioned with his hands, spreading them apart.

"So, the people he stings will be alright?" Amita asked.

"Will anyone be alright?" Tearmai looked at her with his sad eyes.

Amita wasn't sure how to answer. She was thinking about the other word he said, 'causality.'

She was about to ask him what he meant, but then Tearmai continued, "I've been stung by a Hunter before." He pointed to a scar on his side between two armor plates. "See?"

"So, you can help my parents?" Amita asked.

"Maybe," Tearmai answered, nodding. "There is medicine. . . It will wake them. . . I will try to help—I will try to help everyone, but my helping hasn't been . . . very much help."

"Right," Ben said, looking at the diamond. "So how are we going to get this thing in the truck?"

Tearmai lifted the ship again, hoisting it over his head. Awkwardly he climbed into the truck bed, then rested the tip of the diamond on the cab. The back of it hung over the tailgate while the Drake's massive body was completely covered. "I will hold it," he said, peeking out from under the ship. His long arms were squeezing tight to the sides as he lay on his back.

Ben shrugged and looked at Amita. "Looks like I'm driving again."

"We're never going to make it," Amita answered, shaking her head.

# Chapter Thirty-Seven

Katy was frozen, unable to think or move as she stared at this horrible, twisted thing in front of her. "Give him to me," the Hunter said in a voice that sounded like a broken PA speaker, all pops, and crackles, echoing as if from a distance.

Moving slowly toward her its glassy black eyes never left the bundle in her arms. Ten feet away she could still smell the oily substance dripping from its mouth. Its breath was like a car battery melting.

Holding Brash in one hand and the wrench in the other, Katy shook her head and started backing away. She held the tool out behind her, running it along the rail, searching for the wall that would indicate she was by the stairs. The tool was getting heavy when she felt it tap against a power conduit, one of the massive, insulated pipes that held the bundles of electrical wire.

"Give me the Bug!" the Hunter demanded as its bladed arm twisted down. The blade sliced through the handrail, cutting one of the support wires that held the catwalk up. The walkway below Katy began to shake and tremble as the stay wire swung free bouncing off the generators. "Do it now!" the creature commanded, bringing the blade forward to point at her.

Katy looked at Brash, "Can you fly?" she asked. His wings had been damp earlier, that combined with the wind outside had kept him grounded. Brash fluttered his wings and nodded. "Then go!" she yelled, throwing him into the air.

He flew up in an arc like a volleyball. At the top of the arc his wings took over, and he appeared to hover weightless. The light from his body glowed red, twisting with a purple tinge.

"Get to the tunnel," Katy said, pointing toward the door that she'd left open. "Go!"

The Hunter jumped onto the catwalk's handrail, reaching out, trying to skewer Brash. Katy felt a thrill of happiness as she watched the Lightening Bug avoid the swings, ducking and darting.

Brash dove behind Katy to go down the stairs and head toward the door to the conduit tunnel. The Hunter's eyes followed his every move, then glared at her. Katy hoisted her wrench, ready to defend the escaping alien.

Leaping into the air the Hunter stormed forward. Katy's wrench was useless as Pacheco smashed into her, slamming her into the wall. Her head and back crashed against the conduits. She tried to keep her eyes open as she slumped to the floor, struggling to understand what happened.

Katy breathed out, fighting to get air back into her lungs as she watched the Hunter go halfway down the stairs and stop. There was an electrical panel on the wall next to him. He tore its metal cover loose and threw it through the air like a Frisbee at Brash.

The Lightning Bug was nearly at the tunnel when the cover hit him, clipping his wing. A direct hit probably would've cut him in half. He dropped to the ground, skidding to a stop just before the door.

Pacheco, the Hunter, moved slowly, taking his time, going down the stairs. His face was no longer capable of sneering, but his disdain oozed from his toxic voice. "Such foolishness, such a waste," he taunted. "It's no wonder your species is extinct. It'll be my honor to destroy the last of you."

Brash's wings fluttered, trying to get off the ground, but he was stunned and was spinning in a weak circle, unable to get off the floor. After a second, he stopped and turned back toward his killer.

Pacheco stood over him, before the three small steps that led to the tunnel. Behind him, a six-foot wide row of conduits covered the wall.

The Lightning Bug shook his head a little, looking over the Hunter's shoulder. Someone was moving there, and his eyes widened in fear.

Having gotten to her feet, Katy came down the stairs behind Pacheco with her wrench raised high. She smashed it into his back, and the Hunter roared in pain. By luck, Katy's blow came close to where Chris had stabbed the monster earlier.

Pacheco's eyes narrowed as he turned back to her.

She lifted the wrench again, but with a quick slap, the Hunter knocked it from her hand. Slowly his face began to reform. For a moment he was human again, the head of security, although his mouth was still covered with black goo and his body remained a clutter of dark tubes and muscles.

The monster had been bad enough but seeing this awful reminder that he was somehow a twisted form of humanity was even more terrifying. Katy tried to back away, but her foot caught the edge of the stairs. She tripped and fell back.

She struggled to get up as Pacheco leaned down over her, smiling. "Cry for me again. I so enjoyed it the other night after I stung your friend. That's why I kept you in my office so long. Your crying was the best part of my night."

His face was so close to her that every time he spoke, the oil from his mouth dripped on her. Suddenly Katy drove her knee up, hitting him square in the jaw. It was a solid smack, spraying more of that black fluid over the wall, but it only made Pacheco's dark smile turn broader.

He came up the steps laughing as he said, "I know you, girl. You're nothing special. You couldn't be." Then his human face dissolved, splitting and twisting,

"And I've had enough from children for one night." He brought back his arm, the blade extended, ready to slash Katy in half.

Believing her life was over she closed her eyes. Then she heard the buzzing of wings. Even through her closed eyelids, she could sense light, brighter than anything she'd ever known. It was painful and scorching.

There was power behind it. A force that pushed at her and the Hunter. Katy felt her body move, lifted and pulled away from Pacheco.

Brash got to the air flying just above the monster's shoulder. Light burst from him like a star, reaching out with all his will to stop the Hunter from killing her. He pushed Katy free, and for a moment his light filled the air, blinding Pacheco, shoving him too.

Pacheco's incredibly sharp blade descended, coming for Katy until it was halted, lifted by Brash's power. The blade passed over her and kept going through the stair-railing, then on into one of the conduits that lined the wall.

Only the very tip of the cutting edge reached the wires. But it was enough. Pacheco's momentum carried the blade through each piece of insulated conduit, stopping in the last one. The electricity tore through him.

As Katy turned away, she felt the sparks burn her skin. The electricity throbbed, booming in her eardrums. But above all that sound she could hear something shrieking. The Hunter Pacheco was screaming while the current burned through him.

## Chapter Thirty-Eight

Katy opened her eyes, but all she found was more darkness. She ran one hand over the other, not caring for what she felt, patches of tough, leathery skin. They were burns, but they didn't hurt. Didn't feel like anything, numb and tingling a little in places, as if they were asleep. The burn had gone deep enough to destroy the nerves. She could smell charred hair and above that was something worse, a more terrible odor.

Her ears wouldn't stop ringing. She tried to focus, tried to look at her hands, only seeing spots of dark and light. Still, she sensed something moving near her.

"I can't see," she said, reaching forward, not sure who was there.

She sensed the flutter of wings, a buzzing pulse moving the air.

"I can't see!" she said again still reaching out, feeling panicked.

"I'm sorry," an alien voice said. "It was the only way I could help you."

'Was it the explosion? No,' she thought, 'it was the light, that blast of energy Brash had released, just before the thing was going to kill her.' In the distance, she could hear voices. They were calling her name, "Katy! Are you in here?" She recognized Chris's voice.

Her father's voice joined him.

"Your friends are coming for you," Brash said. "Your father must try to close the void space. The power that was containing it is gone. It's already started to expand. It will get worse. It will get worse for everyone if he can't stop it." There was something in the alien's voice that

Katy didn't like, a sort of hopelessness. The buzzing of his wings moved away.

∞

Before the explosion Chris and Alex had left the cafeteria. They couldn't go fast crossing the grounds. Alex tried to push himself, but he was too hurt. He leaned heavily on his brother, gritting his teeth, trying not to let Chris know how much pain he was in with every step.

At least the rain let off. Only the wind remained, though that was violent enough, blowing sand and stinging his eyes. When they finally managed to get into one of the bays at the generator facility, it was a relief. After seeing the headlights from Dr. Virtanen's pick-up, they figured that Katy must've come this way.

It was certainly closer than the observatory, though as he looked at the big open doors, Chris knew it wouldn't be nearly as secure. That creature, Pacheco's alter ego, would go through a garage door without a problem.

Chris helped his brother to the floor just inside the first bay, then went back out to look at Virtanen's truck. It was empty, and the engine was running.

As he stepped back into the bay, his eyes went to the door that led to the generators. It was no longer there, replaced by jagged metal pieces hanging like tissue paper from the hinges. Jake was there though, lying on the ground.

Chris started towards him, searching the rest of the scene. Someone was struggling to get up from behind a workbench. He recognized Virtanen's graying red hair and beard.

"Where is she?" Chris called to Virtanen as he got to Jake and bent down next to him, trying to hear if Jake was still breathing. Thankfully, he was.

"What happened?" Jake muttered, as his eyes fluttered open. There was dirt on the back of his head where it'd been smashed into the wall.

Virtanen pointed at the door. "In there." He staggered over to Chris, bumping into things on his way, trying to stay up while blood seeped onto his face from a wound over his eye.

Chris nodded, rushing through the ragged, rippedup door but he had to stop. Light exploded in front of him. Energy burst against his skin that pushed him back. He turned away, covering his eyes.

As the light faded, there was a boom followed by the crack of something else exploding. When Chris looked up again, he saw the lights in the garage flicker and die.

Through the torn door, he heard the massive generators stutter and cycle down. After a moment they went quiet. A red light over the door flashed while a buzzer sounded. Jake rolled over, trying to get up. "That's not good," he said, grabbing the wall.

Virtanen looked up at the light, then took a moment to glance back at the white dome of the observatory before pushing past Chris. He charged forward through the door yelling, "Katy!" Chris was right behind him.

Inside, emergency lights shone down from the walls on a haze of smoke that hovered just below the ceiling. It was only the height of the room that made it possible to enter and still breathe. Virtanen hurried to the generators, looking around each one to try and find his daughter.

Chris went toward the tool room. He rounded the corner, just in time to see a glowing form go up the stairs. On the floor, something was still burning. It was a massive husk vaguely resembling a person, though most of it had been blown apart, leaving a trail of destroyed flesh halfway across the floor. Little flames burned down weakly on it.

By the stairs, he saw Katy, sitting up with her hands out searching for help. "I'm over here. Dad!" she called as she struggled to her feet.

Chris got to her as Virtanen ran into the room. The scientist grabbed his daughter and pulled her in tight. "Oh, Katy, are you alright? Dear God, look at your hands."

"Is it dead?" Katy asked. "I can't see."

Virtanen glanced at Chris and said, "There was a light in the smoke. Something went up and out the back, over the diesel tanks."

"That's not the dangerous one," Chris told Virtanen. Then he looked at Pacheco's remains. His burnt parts were everywhere. Some appeared human, others were more like a machine. Chris tried not to look too hard, afraid he'd be sick, "It looks like the Hunter's been fried."

Katy's body loosened visibly. Her father held her before she collapsed. After a moment she nodded and managed to say, "Dad, you've got to stop it. . . Your experiment. The other alien, the Lightning Bug, said it would grow unless you shut it down."

Virtanen nodded. "Okay, we'll go do it now." He lifted his daughter in his arms and started back toward the door with Chris behind him.

Jake came around the corner of the tool room as they were leaving. He covered his mouth from the stench and asked, "What the hell happened?"

"The lines have been cut," Virtanen said, motioning back toward the wall.

Jake looked. "That's why the generators stopped. The back surge tripped the shutoffs. This is going to take hours to clean up."

"It doesn't matter," Virtanen said. "I'm calling for a general evacuation." Jake nodded.

"I need one thing from you, though. Get Dr. Wallace. Tell him to meet me at the observatory. Tell him to hurry. Katy is hurt."

"My brother too," Chris said.

Virtanen looked at Chris and nodded, "Get him in the truck. We'll have the doctor meet us there for all of you." He turned back to Jake. "Have security send transports, then get yourself as far from here as you can. It's time to end this."

# Chapter Thirty-Nine

It wasn't easy for Brash to abandon Katy. Seeing the girl scared, alone and blind, her hands burnt so badly, it was hard to leave her, but time was short.

She'd fought to save him, fought with the bravery of the very young, believing she was doing what was right. 'If only they were all this way,' Brash thought.

He wasn't fond of humans. Though his species wasn't actually capable of it, he felt something close to hatred for them.

Such negative emotions were usually inconceivable to his people. His race was too long lived to carry such things. In fact, long-lived beings couldn't indulge in such poisonous thoughts or strong feelings and still last. Hatred was the burden of those bound to die quickly.

Of course, Brash's people could feel concern or a general wariness. That was basic survival. But Brash was more emotional than most of his species. He was young, the last generation born, possibly the last still alive, the sole survivor of a murdered species. He was too young to remember the descent, but these humans would. This would be the generation that would remember their fall, those that survived. They'd go on to create havoc.

Leaving Katy as her friend and her father arrived, Brash had flown up over the catwalk toward the back. The door leading to the diesel tanks was closed, but Brash focused hard, and with a small burst of energy, forced it open. He didn't bleed as much light this time, not using nearly as much strength as he had to save the girl. It'd been a mistake. He'd pushed too far and could feel the void growing.

Flying became easier once he was outside as the storm had already blown through. The wind still gusted but not as violently. He rode the drafts, heading down toward the trailers.

Time was up. He'd failed. He had to admit that. The narrow focus of his actions did nothing to change the direction of the universe. It'd been a long shot, but he had to try. Still, there was something to be taken from all this. He didn't have to give up completely. One mind had been touched among all the ones he'd taken, the best chance of helping on the other side, of finding some way of setting right what was done.

Soon they'd deploy the device. Brash flew through the night without fear, knowing the Hunter was gone. People looked up at the Lightening Bug, but it didn't matter. They were all heading away, escaping what was about to happen. He flew over the facility, came down to the trailers, and hovered over one, sensing the mind inside.

She was still sleeping. That was good. It'd make this easier. He reached out, touching her dreams, sliding into her mind, seeing through her eyes, an odd feeling that required a great deal of focus.

Leaving her bed, the sleepwalker went to the door. Brash looked down at the knob. Doors and walls were bizarre to him. 'It was just like humans to constantly be looking for division, constantly finding ways to isolate themselves, even from each other. Of course, other races built this way too.' Still, Brash thought of them as human things and didn't like them for it.

After some practice, he'd gotten better at using people's hands, at turning doorknobs. So, he reached out with her hand and pulled it open, then walked her to the front. It didn't dawn on him that she was in a nightgown. He had no knowledge of what would be appropriate for a scientist to wear.

He guided her out into the night, then came down over her head, his wings buzzing as he hovered over her. Proximity made his bond stronger. The scientist began to glow, her whole body shining.

He sensed the void space, the opening that these humans had torn in the fabric of space-time. It was growing and expanding. Soon it'd be too late for this world. It would vanish, swallowed whole. Brash had to escape, make his way home to Nalanda, the forever city, and to Altor, the world shepherd.

∞

Katy stumbled, trying to get out of the truck. Chris watched her father carefully take her shoulders and push her back into the seat. "Easy now. Stay here. The doctor will be over soon, but there's something I've got to do."

Katy nodded, but didn't say anything. Virtanen's face tightened as he clenched his teeth. Chris watched the emotion wash over his face as he looked at his daughter's blind eyes, her burnt and damaged skin. The man looked like he was ready to break down. "I've got to fix this," he said. "Keep an eye on her. Dr. Wallace will be here soon with a medical team," he told the boys as he hurried away.

Alex got out, following him, moving slowly till his brother came up next to him.

Virtanen looked back, "Where are you going?"

"I want to see it. I want to know what this was all about," Alex said. His skin was pale, and he looked ready to fall over.

"You should stay here with Katy," Chris said firmly.

Alex stared at his brother for a moment, then he did something Chris had never seen him do. He relented, nodding and settling back into the truck. As he sat, he grabbed Chris's arm. "Fine, but you go with him. Make sure there's no tricks. That this guy does what he says he's going to do. He needs to shut it down."

Chris nodded, then rushed after Virtanen.

Alex watched his brother go. When he disappeared around the corner, Alex looked at Katy and asked, "Are you okay?"

Katy took a long moment to respond. She moved her head around, trying to focus on anything. There was a little bit of light in front of her, spots mostly. "I don't think I am alright," she said, "and I'm really scared."

Alex looked at her hand. He wanted to take it and reassure her, but saw how damaged it was, the way the skin was charred. "It's okay," he said, sounding exhausted and not very confident.

∞

Virtanen and Chris went up the stone steps that led into the science labs. They had left the truck in the garage at the base of the observatory, below the building. Every couple of feet, emergency lights shined down brightly along the long the curving corridor.

They came to a much longer series of stairs, turning back and forth inside a narrow shaft that could be seen from outside, going to the top half of the observatory. The elevator next to it was the preferred way to travel to the observation deck, but with the power out it wasn't an option.

Chris followed Virtanen up to a short corridor with three doors going off in different directions. A uniformed security officer waited there.

"Have them radio and let me know when Dr. Wallace gets here," Virtanen ordered.

The security officer slid a key card over the lock and opened the door. The room they entered was too small for the number of people in it. Computer monitors and other electronic devices covered every surface. On the far wall was a glass window with strange lights shining through it.

The scientists turned toward Virtanen, staring at him and Chris. "Someone give me a damn update," Virtanen demanded.

A man stepped forward, his face pale with a sheen of sweat on his brow. "We don't have any power, the magnetic bubble is gone, and the event is growing," he said in a trembling voice.

"What's the rate?" Virtanen asked.

"Every four minutes it doubles in size and its area of effect grows worse with it." The scientist pointed toward the viewing window and the heavy glass. "It goes through periods of rapid pulsing before each expansion." Chris went to the window and stared out at the inside of the dome.

Understanding the observatory's scale was difficult from the ground. From inside it reminded him of a sports complex like Madison Square Garden. Of course, there were no seats, just massive curving walls with covered walkways running the circumference of the space. Below them, there was no man-made floor. The dome continued down into a sphere with the deepest point carved into the rocky mound the observatory sat on.

As impressive as the room was, it was what it contained that called Chris's attention. He stared at a point in space that seemed to be weeping with color. Bizarre shades that his brain couldn't quite translate moved around a central point, and those colors were like a tidal flow, waving in strange rhythms. He tried to look at the center, but as he did, he felt a pain in his head.

"Do not stare at it for too long. A number of people have developed seizures," Virtanen said from behind him. Chris hadn't noticed till then that the scientist's hand was on his shoulder. "It's a wormhole. Einstein theorized their existence, and I've spent most of my professional life trying to make one that'd be stable and traversable."

Chris shook his head, looking down at the consoles for a moment till the pain cleared. Then Virtanen continued, "Your mother claimed I used a nuclear jackhammer to bust a hole in space-time. I suppose that's a fairly apt description of what I did.

"I didn't give much thought to what we'd find on the other side. There's so much open space. What were the chances we'd find something, contact something? What were the odds? They must've been waiting, those things. It's the only answer. Somehow, they were ready, and they connected at the other end."

Chris could hear the regret in the scientist's voice. Despite the scientist's warning, Chris felt his gaze returning to the window. "Dr. Virtanen, the device is ready," one of the scientists sitting down in front of a bank of screens said.

Virtanen nodded. His eyes went down to a platform that'd been built in the center of the sphere, almost reaching the event. The scaffolding was temporary, made from a metal framework creating a narrow path ending just before the event.

At the end were two men covered head to toe in protective clothing, wearing heavy radiation suits with dark visors. One carried a tough looking laptop that he plugged into a large cylindrical device sitting on top of the platform where the waves of color nearly washed over it. The device was dark, with thick armor plating covering it, and painted on its side was a black and yellow nuclear sign. After the man in the suit opened the laptop, he turned to the observation room giving a thumbs up.

There was a microphone coming up from the console and Virtanen bent down to it. "This is Doctor John Virtanen, authorizing deployment and activation of the thermal nuclear device. Code Omega deployment, initiate countdown." He glanced back at the man sitting in front of the screens.

The man's eyes were on a clock. He waited a moment, then said, "Mark."

Virtanen repeated the single word over the microphone. "Mark." At that moment multiple monitors in the room had clocks appear on them, all of them counting backward from twelve. Chris glanced out the window, watching the men in radiation suits hurry back down the platform.

"That's a nuke?" Chris asked, looking at Virtanen.

He nodded and turned back to the others in the room. "Go ahead and start evacuating. If there's any data to be collected, the monitors can do it on battery back-up."

"That's only twelve minutes," Chris said, pointing at the clock.

One of the scientists who was at a grease board at the back wall had just finished some calculations, taking data from another bank of monitors. "We're good," he said. "The next expansion should place the device just inside the event horizon."

"It's enough time," Virtanen told Chris. "We need to get out of here, but the device itself will have a directed blast. All its force will be sent into the wormhole. Even the radiation will go there. We've found the event tends to trap most forms of harmful energy. I guess that's just another field of study we won't be going into."

The security officer stuck his head in the door.

"Dr. Wallace has the medical team downstairs." Virtanen glanced at the clock. "Good. It's time. Everyone needs to clear out." Some of the scientists were hunched over display screens, and others were copying files onto flash drives. "Alright, I said everyone needs to be leaving!" Virtanen yelled as he went around the room, taking things from people's hands, grabbing elbows and shoulders and pushing them all toward the door.

He came over to the window and took a final look out. Suddenly his eyes widened, and his hand went to his mouth in shock. "Dear God," he said.

Chris was near the door, but when he saw the look on Virtanen's face, he started back toward the window.

"Don't!" Virtanen reached out to stop him.

But it was too late. Chris stared at first, not sure what was bothering the scientist. The alien was there, the flying one that Katy had saved. Brash flew out over the platform, following the walkway.

'He's going home,' Chris thought. 'He's going back through the wormhole before they close it.' Watching the creature, he noticed how its light was brighter than usual, washing in the tidal forces from the wormhole. The colors didn't mix, but seemed to push against each other, the wormhole being much stronger.

The light was so distracting that Chris didn't notice at first that the alien wasn't alone. Someone was with it. Chris's hands tightened into fists when he saw who it was. His mother, in a nightgown with no expression and her eyes glowing. She was bathed in light while her steps barely touched the platform, following just below Brash, going past the nuke, toward the event.

## Chapter Forty

"We've got to stop her!" Chris pulled away from the window.

Virtanen looked at the chamber. Dr. Johnson was halfway down the walkway moving steadily. He glanced toward the clock, which was coming up on ten minutes, almost time for another expansion. The tidal forces around the void pulsed violently. Wind whipped the window as the alien's wings struggled to stay on course.

Chris pushed his way through the crowd of scientists who were leaving.

"Wait!" Virtanen came up behind him. "You can't go out there. You'll never make it in time." Chris was at the door when Virtanen reached out for his shoulder. The security guard was moving back through the scientists, trying to block the way. Just before the entrance the guard placed his hands on Chris's chest.

Chris looked down and felt himself tense up. He wasn't the wrestler his brother was, but he was strong, and he'd gone to enough practices, drilled enough moves that his reaction was swift. He grabbed the guard's arm, pulled it forward while dropping to a knee and lifting him in the air. Chris tossed the guard over his shoulder like a sack of potatoes, flipping him out of his way. Virtanen barely had time to move before he crashed in front of him.

"Stop, it's too dangerous!" Virtanen yelled.

The security officer got to his feet and started after Chris as well, but Virtanen held up his hand. "I'll take care of the boy. I need you to get the rest of these people out of here."

Chris ignored them all, looking down at the key card he'd snatched from the guard's belt. He passed it over another scanner, then ran through a different door, disappearing down a long corridor. Past the doors, Chris saw that the corridor was actually a covered walkway, the one that circled the inside of the sphere. The walls here weren't very thick, only metal sheathing covered in white paint with an occasional window looking out on the event. He glanced out of them as he ran, moving as fast as he could while the strange light reflected off the walls. Every couple of feet a monitor counted down the minutes till detonation.

Through the floor, Chris could feel vibrations. The whole thing, the walkway, the sphere, maybe even the mountain, was moving and shaking. He felt an unfamiliar fear twist in his gut as if he were on the edge of a great depth, ready to plummet, like looking over the edge of the Grand Canyon.

Coming to a set of double doors thicker than the others, he slid the key card through the reader, and they opened for him. He heard Virtanen calling, but didn't wait. He stepped into a room with another set of doors further ahead. These doors were made of tinted glass and isolation suits hung near them. Chris wondered if they'd fit him, wondered if he had time to get one on as he looked out the glass doors. He could see the walkway, see his mother down at the end.

He made certain not to stare up at the event, keeping his eyes on the path and his mother's shadow on the walkway. She looked odd, a squiggle of white with her nightgown dancing around her.

There was no keycard scanner on this final set of doors, only a large red button. Chris pushed it hard, and the doors opened. They slid apart and he rushed forward. The fear became stronger as everything changed. The bizarre light of the void threw his senses into disarray, he was no longer able to tell up from down.

His eyes went to the wormhole. A moment before, he'd been certain it was above him, but now he was just as certain that it was below, like a gaping maw reaching out. He tried to keep his focus on the walkway, but the path moved under him, disturbing his perception. 'Was it coiling in on itself?'

His eyes marched forward till he found his mom again. She was beside the nuclear device with Brash only inches from her head. Chris watched the creature's wings flap as they slowed, becoming visible, then sped up again. Any sense of time was gone. Moments would pass quickly, then become sluggish with the irregular pulse of the light.

The tides seemed to be breaking on his mother. She was glowing in the same shade as Brash. His energy covered her like a cocoon. Chris watched her feet leave the path, climbing or falling toward the event.

"No!" Chris yelled, starting to run, ignoring the odd sensations, focusing only on getting to his mom. Brash looked back at him, but his mother never turned. She rose into the field of light and in a single beat of Chris's heart, disappeared, winking out of existence.

Chris didn't stop. He reached the nuclear device and dashed past it, stepping forward to the very edge of the platform. There was nowhere else to look but the wormhole. "Mom!" he called into the void, feeling tears running down his cheeks. He stared at it, debating whether to jump. Two thick, gloved hands grabbed him. Pulled him back from the edge.

"We've got to go," Virtanen said in a muted voice.
Chris glanced up, seeing a darkened visor. Virtanen was

wearing one of the encounter suits. As he wrapped his arms around Chris's waist and pulled him back down the walkway, Chris did nothing to fight him.

# Chapter Forty-One

The world began to right itself as soon as Chris was back through the glass doors. "It doesn't take much to insulate you from the effects of the wormhole," Virtanen said, taking off his helmet. He touched the doors a moment after they slid shut, "but you have to have something. As you saw, being in the path of those energies can be disturbing."

Chris just nodded. He was slumped on the floor staring right at the wormhole without the headache he'd felt earlier. It was bigger, and its tidal forces seemed to have slowed. They were no longer pulsing as violently. Chris glanced up at a clock that was counting down. It read 7:37. 'Every four minutes it expands.' he thought, remembering the words of the scientist in the observation booth.

"Where did she go?" Chris asked.

Virtanen was pulling the suit off. "To the other side. To wherever those creatures came from. We need to be out of here in case this goes bad."

"Goes bad?"

"We're setting off a nuke, remember?" Virtanen said heading to the door.

Chris still hadn't moved. "You think that'll close it?"

"That's the plan," Virtanen answered. He had the doors open.

"But then she'll be trapped. She'll never be able to come back."

Virtanen turned. "It's growing, Chris. It's not containable. If we don't close it, the result will be more terrible than you could imagine."

Chris looked past the doors. "Could it swallow the whole world?" he asked.

Virtanen took a moment before answering, "We think so, yes."

It was too big, too much to think about. His mom was gone, and Chris had to fight the urge to break down, feeling himself tighten as he shoved the emotion down and nodded, getting to his feet, he followed Virtanen down the passageway. Chris no longer bothered to look at the event. He even tried to ignore the lights as they reflected off the white painted walls.

What he did look at was the countdown displays. The seconds were ticking away. The one in the corridor just outside the observation room read 6:30. Another minute passed before they reached the bottom of the stairs.

They moved through the hallways, coming to the stone steps that led back into the garage. A security officer stood by the door with a counter in his hand ticking off each person as they came out. Above him was one last display on the wall. 4:15. "It's about to grow again," Chris said, pointing at the clock.

Virtanen nodded. "The nuke is timed to go off with the next one."

They exited the garage, looking further through the crowd to see a Humvee with a red cross painted on its side and Katy on a stretcher being loaded into the back. Thick bandages covered her hands. Her eyes had pads over them with white gauze wrapped around her head like a blindfold.

Trails of people streamed out of the observatory's main entrance and from the garage. Chris and Virtanen joined the exodus heading down the road. Chris stayed with Virtanen, noticing that everyone seemed to be looking at the scientist, wondering what could've gone wrong. Ignoring the stares, Virtanen kept his eyes toward the distant sky over the mountains. The clouds from the storm had moved off, making room for the early morning stars to twinkle.

Chris looked from the horizon to the Humvee, hoping his brother was in there and feeling relieved that Alex hadn't been in the sphere with him. He thought of the moment when he stood at the edge of the wormhole, staring into the void. His brother would've jumped, would've followed their mom to who knows where. He remembered the alien light surrounding her and wondered if the energy could keep her safe.

After Katy was loaded in the truck and the double doors closed, the security officer banged on the side, waving for them to move on. The Humvee hurried away toward the medical lab. When it was only a few yards up the road though, just past the first dirt mound, Chris saw his brother looking out the back window, searching through the crowds.

Their eyes met and Alex opened the door, yelling something. Chris couldn't hear him and no longer had the will to hurry, though he felt he should. The Humvee stopped just past the mound and let Alex out.

The vehicle waited there, while Alex looked back at Chris who was shuffling along next to Virtanen. They reached the dirt mound. "It's almost time," Virtanen said staring down at his watch.

Shaking his head, Chris came closer to his brother his sad, tired eyes on the ground. He felt Virtanen lift his arm to check the time again and heard the man count down the last few seconds in a near whisper. "Five, four, three, two. . ."

It was cold. The wind and rain had carried away any of the heat from the previous day. The high desert plateau shivered, and not far away the white dome of the observatory seemed to breathe, letting out a gasp of air. Chris felt it through his feet and against his skin, the shockwave tremor moved through him as the bomb went off. A moment later the sound arrived. The nuclear device exploded like it was underwater, absorbed by the forces, it was trying to destroy. A deep resounding WULMP slapped at their eardrums.

Chris walked up to his brother whose eyes had never left him.

"What's wrong?" Alex asked, overwhelmed with concern, seeing how broken Chris was.

"It's Mom. She's gone," Chris said.

Alex looked at their trailer as Chris grabbed his arm. "It was the alien, the Lightening Bug. It took her through the wormhole. I tried to stop him, but it was too late. She's gone."

"No, that's not possible," Alex said.

Chris nodded quietly. Then his face darkened, and he punched the side of the SUV. He did it again and again, till his brother grabbed him around the neck and pulled him toward him.

Alex hugged Chris. He was struggling to understand through exhaustion and rage what had happened, but he saw how it affected his brother. As he hugged Chris tighter, his hand went to his face, wiping a little at his eye.

# Chapter Forty-Two

'I'm driving an alien in a busted up old pick-up truck,' Ben thought, as he looked ahead at the bumpy road. Every time he hit a hole or a break in the pavement, he'd hear Tearmai groan through the window. Then he'd feel Amita's eyes on him and it was impossible to ignore her look of disappointment. "I'm doing the best I can," he muttered.

At least they were back on paved roads and off the sandy trails in the canyon system. They'd gotten bogged down three times on their way out and Tearmai had to pull them free. The alien never complained, but Ben could sense the creature's frustration.

Once he commented, "The controls for this vehicle seem too big for you." That'd been the second time they'd gotten stuck.

"That's just because you're in America. We like our trucks big here," Ben had assured him.

"Can't argue with that," Amita agreed.

The third time they were buried in sand, Tearmai had grumbled, "Remain seated," as he stood, lifted the Diamond vessel off himself and lowered it to the ground. He sprung from the back, leaving the truck bed bouncing up and down, then heaved the rear wheels clear.

When he plopped back down in the bed, it was with a loud "humph," sound. Tearmai looked through the window, making eye contact with Ben. After that Ben did his best to keep from getting stuck again. They made it out onto the more solid dirt trails, then found the paved road that took them to the main entrance of the facility.

They reached the turn-off for the long private road cut into the mesa and Amita saw the white dome of the observatory. She knew she was that much closer to helping her parents. They still might send her to her grandmother, but at least they'd be alive and awake.

That's all that mattered to her.

She glanced at Tearmai, seeing only the top of his head with tufts of fur blowing in the wind. For the first time since her parents were hurt, she wondered where the creature came from. Before their attack, the thought had consumed her. After, all she wanted to know was whether he could help them.

She watched Ben take the turn toward the facility. As the incline of the hill became sharper, the pick-up struggled under its load. Its engine roared while Ben stepped on the accelerator. After a few turns, a curious sensation settled over Amita.

Something is wrong, she thought, looking ahead.

"That's not good," she said.

Ben kept his attention on the road. "What's not?"

Amita pointed forward. She could see the dome against the night sky, but that was all she could see.

The rest of the facility was dark. "The power's out."

"Yeah, it was out when we left. Remember?" Ben said.

"No, I mean all the power is out now. Look." She pointed ahead. "Something must've happened to the back-up generators."

Amita thought about it for a second. She had her theories about what they'd done here and about all the power they needed. Something catastrophic must've happened if that power had been shut down. Something worse might happen if they didn't get it running again.

∞

There was emergency lighting in the med lab on battery back-up and large, portable LED lamps that glared down on the exam beds. The powerful bluish beams made intense cones of light, while darker shadows formed in the unlit corners of the room. There was sunlight as well, not much, but the early morning was just beginning to swell over the desert. In a short while, the sun would be rising in the east, coming over the mountains.

Dr. Wallace had only a few patients from the evacuation. A man who'd slipped on the stairs and twisted his ankle, and another who needed a nebulizer treatment for asthma. The doctor's main concern was for Alex and Katy. They were across from each other sitting on the edge of their stretchers, looking like combat veterans, bruised, beaten and dirty.

Cursory inspections were given to Chris and Virtanen, who were battered as well. Wallace wanted them to take a bed, but they refused, standing by their family members.

Chris and Alex hardly spoke. Alex was struggling to process what his brother told him. It was about the most bizarre thing he could imagine, that his mother might be dead, or somewhere out in the universe lost on another planet. 'Where do you even start with that? What possible solution was there?'

Alex was laid out holding his stomach where his wound had been re-stitched. The pain was sharp. He had an IV with a button that'd call for morphine if he needed it, but he'd refused to press it, not wanting to become sleepy, not till they knew if the nuke had worked.

Katy's wounds, the burns on her hands, were irrigated and wrapped again with special mesh bandages that could be soaked. The cool water had awakened charred nerves when some of the dead skin was removed, an extremely painful experience. Her arms remained in basins. Wallace would come over and check every few minutes. Her eyes were still covered, and an IV was running into her as well. She would need special treatment in a burn center.

Wallace didn't give her a choice about pain meds. She was floating, feeling relief course through her veins as she leaned against her father while he ran his hand over her back. Chris looked at Virtanen. The man's face was tight with concern. He guessed that it wasn't only for his daughter, but also for the report from the observatory that they were all waiting on.

They could see the dome standing on its pillar of stone through the window, Quiet, serene, there was no sign that a nuclear explosion had just gone off inside.

Virtanen glanced down at his watch. If the blast hadn't worked, they'd know no matter what. With the way the wormhole expanded it'd be close to containment failure soon. 'What would happen then? An introduction of matter such as the ground that sat below the event horizon could drastically increase the rate of expansion.' He thought about the math, thought about the theories, tried not to focus on the horror of what those things meant.

It was a tunnel, he told himself, not a black hole. They hadn't expected it to grow. Sure, it'd been a possibility, given the way they'd artificially expanded it. The introduction of those exotic particles was unpredictable. Maybe there was a tipping point, a place where the expansion would end.

'Still, it'd be too late.' He thought of the western United States suddenly disappearing, then a quarter of the globe. Earth would be thrown off its axis. That'd be enough, an extinction level event.

Through the window he saw a truck moving fast, coming down the road from the facility. That was the inspection team. They were losing time coming to him personally, but communications had gone out when the nuke went off. A low-level EM pulse had fried the command staff's satellite phones and digital radios.

The truck pulled up in front of the med center. "I'll be right back," Virtanen said in a low voice to his daughter as he started for the door. Chris started to follow him, but stopped at the window, watching Virtanen go up to the men. There were two of them, both wearing containment suits with their helmets off.

The man who'd been driving looked at Virtanen and shook his head.

Virtanen ran a hand back through his pale red hair, then turned as if he knew Chris's eyes were on him. The look on the scientist's face wasn't good.

There was a sound, a loud, alarming screech of steel being ripped and torn. Virtanen ducked in fear while Chris heard it through the thick plate glass.

He stared at the dome as its metal skin slowly disintegrated. The structural supports failed from the inside, and piece by piece the outer walls fell into the void. The tidal forces of color and light began to seep out. In only a few moments the whole thing was gone, replaced by something truly strange. A sunrise grew with the center missing, surrounded by colors twisting, swimming like sea life in a coral reef on a stormy day.

Chris felt a familiar fear again, that Grand Canyon tumble in his stomach at the edge of a great chasm.

He turned back to his brother, who'd gotten down off his stretcher, not going far as his IV wouldn't allow him.

"What is it? What's going on?" Katy asked.

Alex and Chris's eyes met, both searching each other for an answer.

"I think it's the end of the world," Chris said in disbelief.

# Chapter Forty-Three

At the main security gate there were lights glowing. Battery backups kept the spotlights alive. The guards had been busy with the evacuation, moving people to a safe distance. Only one was left stationed there, looking down the road, his attention on the approaching headlights of a strange looking pick-up truck.

The truck itself wasn't that odd, but what it was carrying; he'd never seen anything quite like it.

∞

"I don't think he's going to move," Amita said as she looked out the dirty window.

"Don't worry. He's just nosy. You don't usually see a massive diamond on the back of a pickup, pretty much ever," Ben said, tightening his hands on the steering wheel.

"Are you going to stop for him?" Amita asked. The guard was standing directly in the middle of the road.

Ben glanced over his shoulder at Tearmai, seeing the top of his head. The big guy was going to raise a few questions that Ben didn't feel they had time for. "Nah, he'll move." Then quietly he said to himself, "Please move." He looked down at Amita's waist. "Is your seatbelt on?" he asked before stomping on the accelerator.

Amita checked while Ben yelled, "Too late!"

The guard raised his weapon, but he never got a shot off because he was too busy diving out of the way.

The pick-up slammed into the gate. The wire mesh tore loose from its supports, whipping down onto the road, while steel bars bent and twisted denting the truck's bumper and hood. The fence smashed into the roof, breaking the windshield, but Ben didn't let off the gas. The little pickup powered through the wreckage pulling onto the facility's main road.

"You alright?" Ben asked, tapping the brakes a little. He hadn't noticed till it was almost too late that there was a crowd of people milling around the facility. They all stared at the truck, especially the ones who'd almost been hit by it.

"Yeah, I'm fine," Amita answered.

"What about you?" Ben called through the back window.

Tearmai lifted his head and looked in. "You are very dangerous and should not be allowed to control this vehicle," The Drake answered. "Very dangerous," he muttered again, ducking back down.

"Everyone's a critic," Ben said. The crowds started toward them, some interested in the giant strange-looking diamond, and others concerned with the underage driver. Ben kept cruising, saying to Amita, "So where to?"

Amita opened her mouth to answer. She was watching the ground, wondering what would happen next, when she heard the noise. Everyone on the street turned at the same time. No one could take their eyes from the center of the facility on the raised stone platform where the white dome had ceased to exist. The void filled the sky, seeming to float above the mesa.

Amita leaned down looking out the windshield as Ben echoed her earlier words, "That definitely can't be good."

"Yes, very bad," Tearmai said.

Amita turned meeting the creature's eyes. Some part of her understood what she saw there, and it nearly crushed her with fear. She choked it back though and said to Ben, "Take us to the med lab. My parents are there."

∞

It was a struggle for Dr. Virtanen to come back into the med lab. The strange effects of the void space had taken hold outside, changing the perspective of up and down. Time had begun to dilate and retract, each moment feeling longer and shorter, throwing all his senses into disarray. He closed his eyes, fumbling for the door. It helped. Then he felt hands take him and lead him in. The effects remained inside, but not as bad. The thick windows, tempered against the desert heat, offered some protection.

He knew it'd grow worse as the void grew larger. Then there'd be no place to hide. He didn't open his eyes till the door was closed. Chris let go of his arm, staring at Virtanen. "Thank you," he said, making his way to his daughter.

He touched Katy's shoulder. She still looked panicked, sitting up and searching the room for answers with her blind eyes. "I'm back, Katy," he said. "What's happening, Dad? Is it as bad as Chris says?"

Virtanen looked back at the boys. "No, it's going to be fine Lapsi. Everything's going to be fine." He gave her an awkward hug, trying not to knock into her wounds.

Chris went and helped Alex back onto his stretcher while his brother stared at him. Shaking his head without saying anything, Chris let him know Virtanen was lying. Alex grabbed the sides of the stretcher and squeezed. If Katy hadn't been there, Chris thought Alex would've given serious thought to going after Virtanen, maybe even killing him, knowing he was the man who'd destroyed the world. 'It'd probably be doing him a favor.'

'So, do we wait or try to run,' Chris wondered. 'Should we drive as far as we can, see if the expansion stops on its own?' He looked across at Virtanen, wishing he'd give some answers. "Aren't there people you should be calling, like the government?" Chris asked.

It took a moment for Virtanen to answer. "I suppose I should. . . but communications are out."

Chris felt rage building. "Well, we should do something!" he yelled, stepping toward the scientist. Chris had never thought of himself as a violent person, but he was struggling as he tried to comprehend what was about to happen. 'The end of the world!' The words screamed in his head. He looked at Virtanen and couldn't believe the man's arrogance. He thought of his mother, the fear that'd been on her face when she'd learned what they'd made here. How it must've weighed on her.

"Don't do it, Chris. It won't solve anything," Alex said. "We need to put some distance between us and this place."

It was at that moment that a beaten-up truck came skidding to a stop, nearly hitting the med lab door. What looked like a massive piece of glass was sitting on top of it. It took Chris a moment to notice its diamond shape, but by that time, he was more distracted by the large, dark thing with its armored plates that was holding the diamond.

The creature stood to its full height holding the strange artifact on its back. When it turned to glance over its shoulder at the growing wormhole, the colors danced across its beak-like, alien face.

It dawned on Chris that this was the creature from the canyon. He stared at the pick-up, then tried to peer through the window. He wasn't surprised to see red hair on a head that could barely see over the steering wheel.

Carefully the creature lowered the diamond to the ground next to the truck and came around to the passenger's door. Amita held the door partially open, peering over the top. She was staring at the wormhole, her eyes turning glassy as its effects tore into her senses.

The creature was gentle as he picked her up, holding her in one arm, and Amita turned her head into his massive chest by instinct. Then the creature reached its long arm through the cab and tried to grab Ben. But Ben had taken off his seat belt and gotten out of the truck, scurrying away from the outstretched hand.

Ben stared at the void, walking forward without knowing why. He wanted to get closer, feeling a thrill from the tumbling in his stomach. "It's amazing," he said.

Tearmai came around. He was trying to keep his head down, away from the colors and lights. He knew that way led to madness. His massive hand fell on Ben, pulling him in. "Come now, it's unsafe to be out here."

Ben resisted, trying to pull free of the grip, but the creature's strength was unreal. Though he tried to be gentle, the Drake's clawed fingers managed to draw blood, cutting into Ben's shoulder. The pain was intense, especially as Ben tried harder to pull away and dropped to his knees. "Let me go!" he shouted, feeling tears well in his eyes.

"You can't stay out here," Tearmai said, curling his long arm down and pulling Ben away. He headed for the med lab door. Inside he could see the others watching.

Tearmai struggled, feeling the time shifts and vertigo. He placed Amita in the crook of his arm as the door opened, making the way clear.

His eyes squeezed, nearly closed as he came through and placed Ben on the floor and Amita next to him. Virtanen closed the door behind him and the effects faded away. Tearmai breathed out heavily, trying to regain his senses. He opened his eyes. That's when the attack came.

# Chapter Forty-Four

Virtanen knew everything he'd done. He remembered the thrill of discovery back when he worked with Chris and Alex's mom. This had all started then, the creation of the plans that led to what was outside. He fought so hard to find funding, going to private investors throughout the world. It should've been amazing, the greatest leap forward in science since the discovery of the atom. Then it all went wrong.

"You monster!" he yelled as he threw himself at the Drake, his face nearly as red as his beard. "You've destroyed it all." Virtanen shoved at the creature, swinging his fist high, trying to catch him on his beaked face.

His fist landed on the Drake's thick neck where it had all the effect of hitting a rock, leaving Virtanen holding his hand. He looked around the room for something to use and reached for an IV pole, but as he did, Tearmai grabbed the scientist by the arm. He lifted the man off the ground and pulled him closer. "You're the one, aren't you? The cause of all this. You pushed too far. Your time has run out. Even now, you don't know what you've done. What it will reap," the creature said.

Ben's head was clearing from the effects of being outside. He heard Tearmai and in the distance he heard his sister calling, "What is that?" at the sound of Tearmai's strange voice. "What's happening?" she demanded.

Katy had heard the door open and the steps of the Drake, stomping on the tile floor. She could sense the air change outside. Then she heard her father's attack, his yelling. Trying to get up from the stretcher, she nearly fell over. When she felt Chris's hands on her, she batted them away in frustration. "Dad? Are you alright?" she asked.

Ben looked up and saw his father dangling in the air. "Hey, That's my dad. Put him down."

Tearmai stared at Ben. "I am not surprised," he said as he finally let Virtanen go.

Ben came over to him and helped his father stand. "Are you alright, Dad?"

"Someone tell me something!" Katy demanded, pushing her way toward them.

"Katy, I'm fine," Virtanen said, staring at his daughter. Then he shook his head. His eyes went to the floor for a long moment as he exhaled, long and slow. When he finally looked up again, he said, "It was me. You're right. I'm the one who did this. I thought I could control it, but I didn't know." His face was still tight, nearly unreadable.

Tearmai leaned down to him. "You weren't the first, and you won't be the last. Many species have stood at this doorway. Some survive, and some don't." "Will we?" Virtanen asked.

Tearmai stared at him, but he didn't answer. Instead, he looked toward Katy, who was leaning forward with her eyes still wrapped. She'd finally stopped trying to push Chris away. "He's gone, isn't he, my flying friend?" the Drake asked.

"Yes," Chris answered.

"We helped him, and he kidnapped our mother," Alex added with barely controlled rage.

Tearmai nodded, but he wasn't looking at the boys. His eyes were on Amita. "She must've been special. He was hoping to find someone— a mind that could comprehend, that was unafraid to change this."

"I don't understand," Chris said.

Tearmai turned back to the void as he answered, "Maybe she can stop this. . . If it can be stopped." Outside the tidal forces from the void were becoming more violent, rolling and swelling, preparing for another expansion. "Brash will keep her safe. His kind is one of the few that can cross without a vessel."

Just then the ground began to rumble, starting slowly, becoming more violent. They felt it in their feet, the ground rising and falling as the light and color reached out, and the opening doubled in size.

Cabinets bounced open, and supplies fell off shelves while the building shook. Packages of gauze hit the ground and monitors tipped over, going dark. "What's happening?" Katy cried out again. Chris held her steady as the stretcher tried to roll across the floor.

"The tidal forces are touching down. The ground is shaking because it's being torn apart," Virtanen shouted as he came over to his daughter, helping her down.

"Your planet's being swallowed one piece at a time," Tearmai said.

Chris looked up at the opening that had grown much closer to the window. It was just behind the first dirt barricade, a few hundred yards from the med lab. The glass began to vibrate then shatter, opening the room to the madness outside.

Immediately he felt the effects, the sense of falling, the twisting of time. His stomach churned as he tried to look away. He felt his brother's hand on him.

Alex grabbed his elbow and started pulling, pointing ahead toward a door. Chris nodded, reaching back for

Ben and Katy. "Come on," he yelled, but the words were strange. Ben followed, doing everything he could to keep his eyes away from the void. His father and sister where right behind him.

Dr. Wallace was in the room as well, but somehow, he'd fallen, disappearing in the distance as the room twisted behind Tearmai who hurried Amita ahead of him.

The brothers pulled Katy and Ben through the door, then reached back to guide the others into the hall by the cafeteria. The Drake was the last one. He turned sidewise to fit, then slammed the door, shutting out the madness. Everything was strangely calm. Even the building stopped shaking.

Chris peered through the cafeteria window, seeing the wreckage from a few hours before when he and Alex fought the monster. He touched the solid wall behind him, knowing that it'd only protect them for a few minutes more.

'Then what,' he wondered. Maybe they'd be better off just giving up, stop trying to escape and accept what was coming.

Tearmai came over to Chris and placed a massive hand on his shoulder. "There's still hope." He looked up at Virtanen. "The woman, their mother, Brash took her because he thought she could fix this."

"Can she?" Amita asked.

"I don't know. But you'd have to follow them to find out."

"How?" Alex asked.

"The void ship, it's the only safe way through. I've been repairing the seals. It should be able to protect you during the passage. It will be tight, but there's room for the five of you. It fit me after all."

"What about my parents?" Amita asked. "They're in the med lab. Before long those rooms will be gone. What happens when they fall into the void? You can't expect me just to leave them there?"

"You must go! To save your parents and your world— in the void, time and space— all meaningless. Possibilities become endless. It's too much. Only here does each moment count, but they're running out." Tearmai shook his head and clenched his fist, struggling with his words. "Brash explained it, but I— I don't understand. He came here to change things." He reached out for Amita as he motioned toward the others. "Please, you must go. They need you. You don't want to be here for what happens next."

Virtanen was staring at the Drake. The creature stared back. Tearmai wasn't telling them everything.

He wasn't telling them the horrors they'd face here as the Earth was absorbed. A moment after their eyes met, Virtanen nodded and said, "Amita, I'll do what I can for your parents. I'll get them out of there and try to get as far away as possible. I promise."

Amita looked around at the others, Ben, Chris, Alex, and Katy. "You're all going?"

"We have to save our mother," Chris said. "And we're going to do what we can to try and stop . . . all this."

"And I'm going to try to help them," Ben added.

"Your sister is going as well," Tearmai said to Ben.

"I am?" Katy asked. She was holding her wrapped arms in front of her covered face, trying to protect them.

"You are," Virtanen agreed. He touched his daughter's shoulder, staring at her gauze wrapped face.

"Someone needs to watch out for Ben." He turned to Tearmai. "Will they be safe there?"

"There are others there who will help them. . . They are not like you. They are different species, but they're good, kind. They may be able to help heal your daughter's injuries." Tearmai said, staring at Virtanen. He stepped toward the brothers, carefully taking hold of Chris's arm as he leaned down. "There are others who you will have to be careful of, the ones who sent the Hunter." He stood to his full height, adding, "And there's worse still, even worse than that monster." Alex and Chris both nodded their heads.

The Drake turned toward the wall as if he could sense something coming. "We must hurry. It'll grow again soon. It may swallow my ship. Close your eyes. I will guide you." Tearmai was already reaching for the door.

"Wait," Virtanen said. "Come here, Ben and Katy." He pulled his children into him, hugging them tightly.

As he let go, Amita came forward and grabbed Virtanen's hand. "Remember your promise. Take care of my parents," she said.

"I will," he answered.

Alex and Chris nodded to him, neither having much to say as they lined up behind the Drake. Chris placed Amita and Katy in front of him while Ben took the back. Each one placed a hand on the shoulder of the person in front of them. Alex hesitated for a second before laying his hand on the Drake. "I will keep you safe," the creature said, opening the door.

They marched back through the med lab.

With their eyes closed, the effect of the time dilation and retraction wasn't as severe. Of course, closing their eyes only eliminated one sense. To not feel it at all, they'd need to be completely isolated. They wandered toward the void, feeling as if they were hiking down a long shaft.

They could hear Tearmai struggling. He was taking long, deep breaths as he moved forward deliberately, each step considered and slow. Like an anchor, he was something solid for the others to cling to.

It was impossible to know how long it took them to get across the room to the next door. They only knew they were outside in the desert air because it was unnaturally bright. The colors played across their closed eyelids, twisting and turning like it was trying to force them to look. Only the ground below the was solid and the feel of the others with them. When Tearmai said, "We're here," it was like being disturbed in a dream but not quite waking.

Chris opened his eyes for a moment and saw the vessel. The diamond was the only thing that didn't seem to be moving as the colors danced over it. The void was so large that it was impossible to avoid. It swallowed the sky. He watched Tearmai open a panel on the side of the ship. "Quickly," the creature said.

Alex went first, struggling up the side with the Drake's help. He remained standing inside the hatch to help the others. Chris and Ben lifted Amita to him, then guided Katy up.

Ben seemed to freeze, facing the void till the massive hands of the Drake closed around him, lifting him up and dropping him past Alex. The creature was gentler, putting his hand out for Chris.

Chris dropped to the floor, careful not to step on anyone. It was tight inside but still very bright. Each of the diamond panels that'd been reflective from outside was transparent on the inside. There were no seats or cushions, and no apparent controls, only smooth walls and a few devices stored in a bag made for Tearmai. There was a sense the vessel hadn't been made but grown, that they were inside something more like an egg.

Alex helped Chris down, trying to avoid pushing into Katy or crushing Amita. Everyone was squeezed together as Tearmai leaned over the opening. "I will have to guide you while it's still safe."

With that, the creature closed and sealed the hatch. Katy asked, "What does he mean 'while it's still safe?'"

Amita answered, "Each time the void expands, it swallows more mass. He doesn't want us caught in the wreckage."

"Oh," Katy said, "So what's going to happen to him? I mean to put us in, he's going to have to get right up next to this thing." Katy, of course, hadn't seen the void, but she'd felt it pull at her, sensed the way everything seemed to be tumbling down toward it. To her it was a chasm made more frightening for the darkness.

No one answered as they felt the ship lift from the ground. They could see clearly through its sides that Tearmai was below them, his face tightened with strain as he lifted the ship onto his shoulders. He took one step forward and then another, carefully balancing his load.

Ahead, Amita could see the void pulsing again, though soon she could no longer see the sides of the event, only its center. It was fascinating but she turned away, looking at the others with her, Chris and Alex, Katy and Ben. 'Each shared the same feeling of fear, but they had each other,' Amita thought. She turned and stared back at the way they'd come, at the mountains, the sun rising above the distant mesas and then she looked at the wreckage of the med lab where her parents were. 'Will I ever see them again? Was this all about to end she asked herself. Was the Earth going to die?'

Amita's eyes went to Tearmai again. She was thinking about what he said, going over every word as she focused on the sandy soil beneath the creature's feet. He took another step and then there was nothing beneath him. The ship floated away from his shoulders, slipping off into the void.

# Epilogue

The colors twisted on the edge of forever, dissolving into blackness. Closing their eyes was the only choice as the walls of the diamond vessel filled with things their perception couldn't handle. They huddled close together, feeling the ship drift aimlessly. Each moment was carved grudgingly from forever as they fell, slipping in the wake of forces they couldn't understand. They held tight to each other, their flesh the only thing that felt real, struggling not to look.

Something solid bumped them, and they woke from a dreamless sleep that they hadn't known they were in. It was outside. It touched the hull. Chris opened his eyes to see red flames dancing across the glass. He felt a sudden jarring lurch as the ship pulled away from the void toward the night sky.

Ben, Amita and Alex, all looked confused, staring up, seeing a glittering field cut by wide bands. Past it were the stars. Without being aware of it, Chris had placed his hand on his brother's shoulder and closed his fingers around Amita's hand. Ben had taken his sister in his arms, reaching out to touch Amita as well. Under any other circumstance the five of them would have been embarrassed by their closeness, but in such a strange place, looking out, the only hope they had was in each other's touch.

Ahead of them was another spot of burning flame carrying something else against the starry background.

It was a body, the limp form of the Drake.

They came closer to the glittering field and saw it grow larger, pulling apart and separating into particles, large chunks of ice and rock.

Chris felt as if he were being pushed on as they rose. It was the force of inertia asserting itself, driving them back into the wall of the ship. Ben placed his hand against it, touching where the flames were. They moved like liquid over the surface, wiggling around his fingers. He was looking out toward the body of the Drake when Ben spoke. "Do you think he's alive?"

"I don't know," Amita responded. "I don't see how, if that's hard vacuum out there." She was just about to touch the side of the ship as Ben had, but she hesitated. "I don't know what this stuff is, but it looks like it's covering him." Her mouth moved oddly under the constant pressure on them.

The feel of being pushed, shoved into the back wall was constant and getting worse.

Chris stared at the Drake, floating there, covered in light then looked past him. There was something out there, floating in the field, different from the rocks and ice. A dark mass with small lights glowing from it. "What is that?" Chris asked. His eyes stayed focused on the object as it became clearer and larger while they approached.

Soon they saw that it was a place, only partially made from the rock of an asteroid. With towers, columns, and bridges, it looked like a city, ancient and pitted with wear, somewhere between a futuristic metropolis and a medieval castle. Chris turned back to look at the void below him, not sure how far away it was, but knowing they'd traveled a great distance. The void space seemed to be dropping, enveloped by tangerine clouds. "Is that a storm?" he asked.

"I think it's a planet, a gas giant," Amita said pointing off in the distance. "There's the horizon." A star shone over the thin curved line, brightening the sky. It was stretching and lengthening almost as if it had a tail. After a moment, Chris realized the star wasn't alone. A second bright point was casting its own light over the horizon.

"Two stars," Chris said, watching the energy from the celestial bodies mixing together. Beyond the city, half in shadow, half in the light of the newly risen suns was a tiny blue marble hovering in orbit.

"Another planet?" Chris asked.

"A moon, circling this world," Amita motioned with her head toward the gas clouds below them. "And this debris field is a ring, like the ones that circle Saturn."

"We're moving." Ben stated the fact that everyone else was aware of.

Amita reached out for the glass wall again. This time she touched where the flames clung to the side of the ship. "Some sort of propulsion," she said to herself.

Ben's hand was still there, "Cool, right?" he asked. The energy danced between their fingers as it carried them closer and closer to the city.

Katy cried out in the back, whimpering. "It's too much," she said still trying to keep her arms from touching anything. Right then, as if in response to her pain the ship slowed.

Ahead, they could no longer see the whole of city as it dominated their field of vision. There were lights on, glowing points like the windows in any other city, but many of the towers were dark and forbidding.

They came near a platform at the edge of the city, rising above it for a moment, then slowly descending onto what appeared to be a massive ledge paved with flagstones. The diamond vessel was placed between five statues. They were dark, and not very detailed, barely resembling a person. Chris thought of the ancient bodies caught in the volcanic explosion of Pompei, covered in molten rock and frozen for all time. That's what these statues reminded him of.

He watched the flames leave the side of their vessel, lift into the sky, then come down on top of the statues, disappearing into them. The heads of the statues began to glow like the embers of a dying fire. A single spot, a point in the center of each head burnt the brightest. Those points seemed to be looking at the diamond. Then the statues began to move, taking slow, loping steps that became more assured as they approached the group of travelers.

Rock hands reached out to touch the diamond. They lifted as a team, bringing the vessel up and placing it on their shoulders. They began to march toward a set of massive doors. One statue remained behind to lift and carry the Drake over its shoulder.

Chris could feel the vibrations as the doors opened, pulling apart.

Amita noticed something else. During their rise from the gas giant, she'd felt the pull of inertia, but now she felt a more subtle force telling her which way was down. It was gravity, or something that gave the illusion of it.

They were carried forward into a large dark chamber. Blue lights pulsed around the floor as the statues lowered the ship to the ground. There were vibrations again as the doors closed behind them, blocking out the light reflected from the gas giant.

"What do we do now?" Chris asked, looking at his brother and Amita. They were both staring at the chamber and the living statues that'd carried them in.

"Get out, of course," Ben said, his hand going to the hatch.

Chris grabbed Ben's arm. "Hold on. We don't even know if there's air out there." Just then another large door opened. Chris looked up toward the other end of the chamber as several figures stepped into the doorway. Lights shone behind them, hiding details and making silhouettes.

One stepped forward, an old man with a beard, obviously human.

"He's breathing," Ben said as he released the lock on the door and pushed open the hatch. He climbed out, jumping down to the floor while trying not to land on one of the statues.

Chris followed him. He stood on top of the ship, looking down at the statues with their one glowing eye. One of them seemed to be reaching out to him, willing to give him a hand climbing down. "Um, that's okay. . ." Chris started to say, but he stopped, hearing a loud shuffling noise from the direction of the massive open door. He turned, looking past the old man toward the entrance that was now blotted out by shadow. Something big stepped forward, over ten feet tall and leaning on a staff. Hanging from the large piece of wood was a small lantern.

It was a Drake, far larger than Tearmai, the one they'd known, the one that was being gently laid on the floor. This new arrival's bony protrusions were longer and gnarled, and its scales were darker. Its tufts of hair were white and gray, some braided with beads, hanging between its armored skin.

"Would you look at the size of that guy?" Ben blurted out, starring up at the massive creature. It took another step forward as Ben held up his hands and shouted for all the creatures to hear. "We come in peace."

The Drake's sharp gaze went between Chris and Ben while its lantern glowed brighter, pulsing with energy. Chris felt it touch him like an icy wave as in a deep, rumbling voice, The Drake said, "This is strange, very strange."

Chris looked at the lantern and saw something there. It was a Lightning bug, like Brash, trapped in amber.

Pete A O'Donnell is the creator of Illadvisedstories.com, a children's story podcast where kids can listen to free and funny tales. He is a firefighter and EMT in his day job and holds a degree in Journalism and creative writing from Queens University.

His first novel, The Curse of Purgatory Cove won the Royal Dragonfly award for best new author. The Stars Beyond the Mesa is his third novel and the first in a seven-book series.

If you're interested in seeing character designs from this book or learning about all the species and worlds in book two, The Ocean Beyond then go to PeteAODonnell.com to receive your free character guide.

38034728R00144